ABOVE
THE STORM

Above The Storm

Cover Design by The Book Brander
TheBookBrander.com
Content Edits: Sue Brown-Moore
SueBrownMoore.com
Copy Edits: Laurel C. Kriegler
laurelckriegler.wordpress.com
Print Formatting by Nina Pierce of Seaside Publications
NinaPierce.com/book-formatting/

First Edition
ISBN: 979-8-9867802-0-7

ABOVE
THE STORM

SILVERSTAR MATES

INTERGALACTIC DATING AGENCY

USA TODAY BESTSELLING AUTHOR
LEA KIRK

SFR by LEA KIRK

The Prophecy Series
(in chronological order)

Prophecy
Book One

Blue Christmas
A Prophecy Series Holiday Novella

Space Ranger
A Prophecy Series Short Story
(*newsletter exclusive*)

All of Me
A Prophecy Series Short Story

Salvation
Book Two

Collision
Book Three

Skylar's Gift
A Prophecy Series Novella

Paradox
(Coming Soon)

Silverstar Mates Series
(in recommended reading order)

Fly With Me
Above the Storm
Wing and a Prayer
Trial by Fire

PNR by LEA KIRK

Made for Her
Part of S. E. Smith's, The Worlds of Magic, New Mexico

ONE

─────────✦─────────

What is a love match? Kyzel Raptorclaw stared at the projection of the mate matching application that hovered in the air over the table in front of him. A monarch should know, should understand, but this was beyond his experience.

He shifted his backend to ease the ache from sitting too long on the coved wooden perch. Careene had known—on some level, at least. And it had resonated with her enough to pluck a death-bed promise from him.

"Your next mate, Kyzel, choose her for love, not duty or tradition. Swear it."

He had so sworn. There had been no other choice. After more than thirty-seven sun migrations together as co-monarchs of the raptor clan, he could not let her soul pass into the Great Aerie in anything other than a state of peace.

It was now nearly one long sun migration of mourning and secrets since her passing.

"Are you sure you must do it this way, Kyzel?" The question came from the male at the opposite end of the long wooden council table.

He raised his gaze to meet Rol's eyes, one gray one blue—a unique and unfortunate combination for a raptor. His childhood friend, and full-time prime advisor, understood the reasons behind his subterfuge, but had reservations. Heavens, he had reservations, yet he must follow through. It was a sin to disregard a deathbed vow.

"Do you know a better way to both keep my promise and fulfill the law?" Because the law for surviving monarchs was clear: a sun migration to mourn, another sun migration to find a new mate and co-ruler.

If he did not fulfill the law, he would be replaced as the elected leader of the raptor clan. In short, he would betray the confidence of his people. Yet, fulfilling his promise to Careene could very well disturb the fabric of Bezchian society. No, not could... would. Once the elders found out, they would protest.

It was not his intent to undermine the immortal mate-matchers of the Firewing clan, but they did not make matches for this elusive emotion called love. Their matches were made based on logic and the strengthening of the families. It was a sacred duty they performed for the four mortal clans, and they took it very seriously.

Rol shook his head, the silvery streaks through his dark headfeathers catching the light from the ceiling fixture as he did so. "I had hoped that during your time of mourning, a better air current would open to you than the services of an agency founded by an off worlder."

So did I.

He scrubbed his hands over his face. "The Silverstar

Agency has an excellent reputation for love matches. Their success rate rivals that of the elders."

"The elders did well by you and Careene."

True. Both of them had had the desired strengths of character to lead their clan, and, by law, no monarch could rule alone. So, they had entered into a mating union together, provided six heirs for the Raptorclaw clan, and led their people in harmony and prosperity.

Kyzel rested his forearms on the table and let his wings droop a fraction under the weight of the truth. "As fond as we were of each other, it was never a love match. And that is what she wanted for me."

"But, does it have to be Earth?"

There were many other planets in the Galactic Alliance of Planets to choose from, but something about the obscure little planet appealed to him.

A chuckle rose up. "Honestly, Rol, you have already admitted several times that such a match might help solidify our relationship with Earth. It is largely due to your efforts that the Bezchi Intergalactic Trade Guild has finally reached out to them with a request to open negotiations."

Rol fluffed the feathers of his mighty wings and made a harrumph sound. "Only because Captain Sovah's Earthling mate would not stop beating her wings at me."

He gave an amused huff at the turn of phrase. "Ava does not have wings."

"And that's is another issue," Rol raised one finger and shook it in his direction. "Humans have no wings, or even talons."

As illustration, Rol extended and retracted the claws embedded in the tips of his fingers.

"Her lack of wings, and the presence of finger and toe nails, does not seem to have affected Sovah's feelings for her." The older couple had been a mated pair for over fifteen sun migrations, ever since Sovah had discovered and freed the human female from an illegal slave ship.

Admit it—they have something you and Careene never had.

Something the elders had refused to acknowledge. He tapped one finger against the opposite forearm. Could Careene's close friendship with the captain and his mate be why she had made her request?

"You know," Rol said tracing a design across the tabletop with one finger, "it is not too late to have the elders match you with a younger mate who could provide more heirs."

Anger swelled in his chest. He slapped his palms against the table and rose, unfurling his wings almost fully. "Again, no." How many times did he have to say it? "At sixty sun migrations, the last thing I need is a new brood of fledglings to chase around. I have done my duty to Bezchi in that department, Rol. Have you?"

Red colored Rol's face from pointed peak of his headfeathers down to his chin. His friend drew his wings close to his back and dipped his head in a show of submission. "I have served our clan and Bezchi by serving you and Careene, Kyzel."

Shame washed away the anger, and Kyzel blew out a gust of air. It was not Rol's fault he was unmated. "I did not mean to devalue your contribution, my friend. Forgive my words spoken in haste and frustration."

The stress of this decision must be weighing heavier on his wings than he had realized.

He shoved his fingers through his headfeathers. "I do understand the sentiment you are trying to convey, Rol. I truly do. I do not seek to disrespect the elders; they are vital for the continuation of our society. But I have done my duty to all, as did Careene. We have assured the future of our clan, and our world, with more than enough heirs. I have no desire to enter another arrangement with a younger, fertile female. Bezchi has what it needs from me. It is my turn to find a female of age with me to share what remains of my time this side of Aerie."

The final choice was up to his mate, of course—whoever she was. And rejection was always a possibility. A ripple of unease shivered through his wings as he returned his backend to the highly polished perch. This would be a quest of faith, one in which he would put his trust in others he did not know. Others not from Bezchi.

"You spoke to your heirs, then?" Rol's question broke through his thoughts.

"Yes. They are all in support of my choice." Especially the youngest three, who were not yet mate matched.

"Then by all means, submit the application now before the rest of your advisors arrive. They will be here soon."

He shifted his gaze to the projected document and tapped the fuzzy outline of the icon marked Submit at the bottom. The image blinked out of existence and another took its place.

> Application and bio-sample accepted. The Silverstar Agency thanks you for your application. You will be contacted by an agent for an interview. Your agent's name is Ms. Nixy Vogel.

"It is done." A deep sigh slid out. "Do you still plan to make the journey to Earth with me once a match is found?"

Rol nodded. "With any luck, the Trade Guild will have progressed to the negotiations stage with the humans by then. It would give me an opportunity to sit in on a session or two."

The soft sigh of the doors opening to admit his lesser advisors, Kopa and Vyat, ended their private conversation. Kyzel waved his hand through the projection of the Silverstar confirmation and it dissipated from view.

"Greetings, my monarch." Kopa—Rol's presumed successor when his friend eventually stepped down—bowed her head in his direction.

Vyat mimicked her action, dipping his featherless head.

"Greetings, Kopa, Vyat." Kyzel inclined his head as each took a seat on the backless perches on either side of the table.

It had been the four of them since Careene's passing. An even number—which was risky if they split on a vote. That had not happened yet, but could change today depending on how well he presented the situation at hand. And if he could convince them he was not in the beginning stages of the mindlessness. Thankfully, the cognitive-stealing condition did not normally affect one of only sixty sun migrations, and there was no history of it in his lineage.

"Thank you for your attention today." He paused as they

murmured the appropriate responses. "My sun migration of mourning is near an end, and I have much to tell you about our future. I request you hold your comments and questions until I have laid out my plan."

Kopa and Vyat exchanged a brief glance, then refocused their curious gazes on him. He presented them with what detail they needed from his death bed promise to Careene.

"Rest assured, my advisors, I do not make this decision lightly. After extensive research, I have determined two facts. First, though smaller and wingless, we all know that the humans of Earth are compatible with Bezchians. Second, the Silverstar Agency has a nearly perfect love-match success rate. What remains is will you support me in this endeavor?"

Silence weighed heavy in the room, which was better than he had hoped. At least neither of them had jumped off their perches to shout him down as some sort of winged abomination. Or worse, a traitor.

"My monarch." Vyat tilted his head to one side. His crown was topped with smooth, leathery red skin instead of headfeathers. "I am not unsympathetic, but do have my reservations about this plan."

Kyzel flicked his gaze to Rol and back. "You are not alone in this, Vyat. Even I have reservations. However, after nearly a full sun migration, no better plan has presented itself. Unless you have one."

"If only I did." Vyat sighed. "Still, it is my advice that you refrain from this action and have the elders find you a new mate."

"I disagree." Kopa's caramel headfeathers framed her heart-shaped face and round golden eyes. Her kind were one of the few raptors with night vision. "Our monarch has served us well. I say that he has more than earned the right to such potential happiness, as unconventional as it may seem."

A chuffing sound of disagreement rattled in Vyat's throat. "The tradition of mate matching has also served us well, for many thousands of sun migrations."

"True." Kopa nodded. "Yet, would you agree that without the support of his advisors, Monarch Kyzel will be unable to fulfill Monarch Careene's final wish?"

"I do agree."

"And that failure to not at least attempt to do so will be a sin upon his soul, which could deny him entrance into the Great Aerie?"

Vyat shifted in his seat and lowered his gaze to where his folded hands rested on the table. "Yes."

The poor bird was as conflicted as the rest of them.

Rol's huff drew Kyzel's attention back to the opposite end of the table. "As we are all aware, the Silverstar Agency has a nearly perfect success rate."

Kyzel gave his head a single slow nod. Where was Rol going with this flight of thought?

"Then, there is a small chance this match will fail. If it does, will you agree to turn to the elders and accept a Bezchian mate?"

That was more than fair. "Yes, I will agree to this."

"Then you have my support, my monarch."

Satisfaction flashed in Kopa's eyes as she turned to Kyzel. "You have my approval as well, my monarch."

"Which leaves me." Vyat chuckled and made a shrugging

gesture with his hands. "Despite our current even numbers, we do not seem to be in danger of a split vote. You have my support, my monarch, although I still have reservations. But the future is unwritten, and I look forward to meeting your new mate."

Kyzel dipped his head in gracious acknowledgment. "I am humbled by your support, my advisors. Rol, will you oversee announcing our plan to our clan?"

The sooner word got out, the sooner he could address his peoples' questions and concerns. It would be reassuring to have most, if not all, on his air current before Silverstar located his mate.

I hope you are right about this, Careene.

TWO

———✦———

"I can't believe you talked me into this crazy idea, Meryl." Robyn Martin Donahue stared at her cell phone as if it had a contagious disease, even though it looked so innocent laying there on the kitchen counter. "Why am I even listening to you?"

She shifted her gaze to her best friend perched on the stool next to hers.

"Because you know I'm always right." Meryl took a sip of wine. "And because you deserve to have a guy in your life who will treat you right."

Okay, that might be true.

Beyond the kitchen window screen, the late summer night was alive with crickets and young party goers hanging out at the park across the street. But in the tiny, well-lit kitchen of her mid-twentieth century bungalow, it was just her and Meryl, having their weekly wine and whine session.

"But, dating an off-worlder?" Funny how that sounded better outside her head. Like maybe this idea wasn't as crazy as she'd first thought.

Meryl barked a laugh. "I think we can both agree that Earth guys haven't exactly panned out for either of us."

That was true. Kevin had been a verbally abusive mega control freak. He still was, with his weekly "check-in" phone calls. Gracious, how had she managed to live thirty-five years with the guy and not suffocate him with his pillow?

"Besides," Meryl continued. "You deserve someone who doesn't *mysteriously* bolt after a couple of dates."

Not this again. Kevin wasn't the reason she couldn't seem to keep a guy around. If anything, it was her expectations that scared them away. Yes, she could do better than her ex, and a couple of times she'd thought she had. Too bad none of the handful of guys she'd dated in the last five years had felt the same about her.

But Meryl wasn't going to distract her with that old disagreement.

"All right." She straightened her spine and adjusted her black-framed glasses on her nose. "I'll submit an application… *if* you do too."

Meryl's hazel eyes widened. "*Me*?"

"*Yehhsss*, you." Because what off-worlder wouldn't want to date Meryl? She was tall and slim, and had been mistaken for Michelle Hurd more than once. *The complete opposite of my pale, blonde, frumpy, librarian-in-a-sweater look.* "C'mon, Meryl. Ya know you want to."

"Date, yes." Meryl frowned critically at the final centimeter of wine in her glass, then slid it toward Robyn over the Formica countertop. "Date *off-worlders*, not so sure. Hit me."

Robyn grinned and tipped the bottle. Meryl was stalling

and soon would cave. The merry chug of liquid was a promise by the crisp white wine to help deliver her friend's consent. "Think about it this way: you won't have to sleep with every man on the planet to prove your theory that all Earth guys suck."

Meryl sniffed. "Maybe I want to."

Darn you, Nathan for screwing with Meryl's mind like that.

"Oh, please. I know you better than that." Robyn topped off her own glass and set the bottle down with a clunk. "Unless you think you're too old for online dating."

"I'll have you know, my dear Robbi, that the Silverstar Agency is a successful and reputable matching company." Meryl tapped one finger against the stem of her wine glass. "And sixty-three is not too old."

Kind of her not to point out that fifty-nine wasn't either. "You're avoiding the question."

Her friend pushed out her full lips in a pout and glared at her wine glass. The cricket song from outside seemed to pick up, filling the silence in the warm kitchen.

"Meryl?" Robyn dragged out the *l*.

"All right, fine. I'll do this with you." Meryl reached for her own cell phone. "What could go wrong?"

A few possibilities leaped to Robyn's tongue, possibilities that might give Meryl reason to back out. Not the least of which was that things might work out so well between her friend and some unknown off-worlder, it'd put an end to Meryl's revenge-sex cycle.

"Okay," Meryl said. "I'm ready."

That fast? "Did you... you already filled it out, didn't you?"

Meryl grinned. "I know you better than that, too."

A laugh burst out of Robyn. "I guess so. Okay, then, application first, then we do the bio-scan app." She raised her phone to chest level and peered through the bifocals at the screen.

The *Submit* icon blinked temptingly, like a beacon to a lonely sailor.

Meryl met her gaze. "Ready?"

"I'm ready."

"In three…two…one…go."

Once the application and bio-scan had been sent, Robyn blew out a long breath. A sense of giddy anticipation curled in her gut as if she had done something very naughty. And in a way, she had.

"So." Meryl set her phone on the counter. "That's done."

"Yep." Robyn nibbled at her bottom lip. "How long do you think it'll take?"

"Hopefully a while." Meryl shrugged her slim shoulders. "I'm not ready for some virile old guy to haul you off to his planet, yet."

"*Ha*. Is there a such thing as performance enhancers for off-worlders?"

"No idea." Her friend waved one hand. "As long as they've ironed out that four-hour-erection ER-visit issue, I'm good. I wonder if the time is doubled if they have two dicks?"

This time Robyn doubled over, wrapping one hand around the seat of the backless stool to keep from falling off as laughter shook her.

One thing was for sure, no matter how long it took, she and Meryl would have fun speculating.

Two months, and still no word from Silverstar. Robyn tapped the end of her pen against her desk as the young woman on the other end of the phone chattered excitedly in her ear. It was a good thing she had her job to distract her during the day. Despite the stress from the divorce, and the necessity for her to return to the ranks of the full-time employed, landing the job as a case manager for Safe Harbor Women's Advocacy Group had turned out to be one of the best things to ever happen to her. It wasn't a glamor position, but it was more than she'd thought possible back in her stay-at-home-mom days.

"Thank you so much, Robyn," the young woman gushed. "I couldn't have done this without you."

"My pleasure, Sasha." Robyn said her good-byes, then placed the receiver of her work phone in its cradle. "Next to raising my kids, this has to be the hardest, and most rewarding, job ever."

Her supervisor grinned. "The Sasha Townsend case?"

"Yeah." Sasha, a young woman the same age as her youngest daughter, had three kids all under the age of six. "She just landed a job with a tech company. They're giving her day care and flexible hours, *and* offered to help with her tuition."

Some days you just won the lottery.

Jayla pumped her fist in the air. "Hell, yeah."

"Doesn't get much better." She glanced at the old industrial analog clock on the wall. "Nice to end the week on a high note for a change."

"Nothing better. Got any big plans this weekend?"

"Nah." Didn't she wish, though.

Face it, Robbi ol' girl, you were hoping to be snuggling with a hot off-worlder by now.

She'd given up stalking her cell phone for a text or email from Silverstar weeks ago. The only time it was out of her purse recently was for work-related reasons, or to text Meryl.

Maybe she really was too old for online dating. But fifty-nine didn't *feel* old. If it was, the agency would have told her by now.

"Um, Robyn," Jayla said. "Your phone's buzzing."

The faint hum came from the direction of her bottom desk drawer. "Oh, shoot. Thanks."

Must be Meryl checking in for tonight's wine and whine date. She yanked the bottom drawer of her desk open, and the loud screech of metal on metal filled the tiny, mostly empty, office.

"*Gah.*" Jayla covered her ears.

Robyn gave her boss a sheepish look. "Sorry."

Someday, Safe Harbor might be able to replace the original circa-1980s desks, but probably not before she retired.

Buzz.

She delved her hand into her purse, her fingers wrapping around the humming device before pulling it out and holding it at arm's-length.

It was not Meryl. "Well, it *was* a good day."

"What?" Jayla's concerned expression was heart-touching. "One of your other cases?"

"No." She gave the phone a severe frown. "Kevin."

"Oh." Jayla nodded. "Shit. That asshole just doesn't take

a hint, does he?"

"No, and it's not for lack of trying."

Buzz.

Jayla turned back to her desk. "Good thing you don't have plans this weekend."

"What do you mean?"

Her boss gave her the "you know darn well what I mean" look.

Why did everyone seem to think Kevin was the reason she hadn't been able to keep a guy around for longer than a month? Like she owned zero responsibility for what happened to her? Real life didn't work that way, and she wasn't perfect. If she had been, she wouldn't have waited until her youngest daughter graduated college to walk out on him.

Buzz.

You were a coward, using the kids as an excuse. In retrospect, leaving when they were young might have been better than trying to keep up the "happy little family" pretense.

Yep, less than perfect.

"You going to answer it?" Jayla's question brought her back to the moment.

"Yeah." She heaved a sigh and tapped the screen. "What?"

"Hello to you too, pumpkin."

Oh, look. It's Sweet Kevin. "Hello, Kevin."

"How was your day?"

"It was going great." Get to the point already.

"Mine was rotten, until I heard your voice."

Ho, boy. "Thank you?"

"What are you doing tonight?"

"You know, instead of trying to live vicariously through me, you really should get out and meet some other women. You know…go on a date."

"There's never been anyone—"

"You *know* where I am every Thursday, Kevin."

Her ex made a scoffing sound. "With Meryl."

Wow. For once he didn't say Can't-keep-a-husband Meryl. "Yes. With Meryl."

"Did you leave me because you went lezbo with her?"

What the ever-loving…? Sometimes the man was enough to make her want to swear. "Good bye, Kevin."

She lowered the phone and press the end-call button. "Pizzle brain."

Jayla snorted a laugh. "Wow. That was bad enough for you to resort to Shakespearean insults. Do I want to know?"

"Probably not. No sense in him ruining both our evenings."

She dropped her phone into the depths of her purse. It could stay there until Monday, for all she cared. She went through the motions of shutting down her computer, locking up her desk, and wishing Jayla a nice weekend. Home was where the peace was, and she couldn't get there fast enough.

THREE

---✦---

Silverstar Agency offices.

Kyzel gazed out the second-floor window of his case manager's—Ms. Vogel's—office at the human colony... *city...* below. The humans of Earth had some unusual concepts in habitation. Mingling their business centers and their family nests in the same colony was unlike anything he had ever imagined. It had always seemed less crowded—and more restful—to have them separated, as on Bezchi. Although, there were advantages to grouping them together as the humans did.

All the differences aside, it was good to finally be here, with his bodyguard, Fyad and Rol in tow. Word of his match had come shortly after he had secured the official support of his clan. Most of them, at any rate. Careene's flock had grumbled, but Rol—ever the negotiator—had appeased them with the promise to personally vet Kyzel's new mate.

As if conjured by his thoughts, Rol appeared at his side, his wings drawn in close to his back as he studied the activity on the street below. "I do not understand the use of the

18

automobiles here. Humans may not be able to fly, but if they created smaller colonies, they could simply walk from place to place. Like our Landwalker clan."

"True. Yet their ingenuity has helped them make up for their lack of wings."

Rol grunted in a noncommittal sort of way. This process would be far more agreeable if Rol had simply joined the Bezchian Intergalactic Trade Guild on their pre-negotiation, introductory tour of Earth. The negotiations would be held afterward in Los Angeles, a city purported to be nearby. Alas, the stubborn old hawk had insisted upon accompanying him to the Silverstar offices instead.

The office doors slid open with a swoosh behind Kyzel, Ms. Vogel hurried in, white papers fluttering in her hand. She was a medium-height female for an Earthling, which put the top of her head barely as high as his chest. She appeared roughly five or six sun migrations younger than himself, with *hair*—not headfeathers—of a vibrant deep red tone. Headfeathers of brilliant colors were common to some clans on Bezchi—particularly the Firewing clan—but she was the first human he had seen with such a color.

She breezed past Fyad—standing guard like a shadow just inside the doors, alert even in the privacy of the agent's office—and sat in the cushioned black *chair* behind her desk. The piece of furniture was similar, yet different, to the perches on Bezchi. Its high, wide back was not built to accommodate Bezchian wings.

My future mate will need such chairs *for her comfort.*

"Sorry for the delay." Ms. Vogel tapped the bottom edge of the pages against the top of her desk. The resulting crack of the impact seemed hollow in the office space. "I have your updated contract, with the specific consideration we discussed." She fixed him with a skeptical look. "Are you sure you don't want your match to know about your royal status?"

Rol folded his arms over his chest. "That is non-negotiable."

Ms. Vogel bit her bottom lip, then nodded. "Well, I can't say I agree, but Silverstar will honor your wishes."

Kyzel dipped his head in acknowledgment. "I thank you for your discretion."

This could very well backfire. But Rol had insisted he would not be at peace unless he was certain Kyzel's future mate loved *Kyzel*, and not the royal title that would be hers, should she agree to mate with Kyzel. It was a fair and persuasive argument.

Ms. Vogel slid the papers across the desk. "For your convenience, I had my assistant translate the contract into Bezchian for you."

"I am honored." His internal translator would have automatically deciphered the English lettering, but he was grateful for how thorough and obliging the agency had been thus far.

"Take your time reading it, then sign at the bottom." Ms. Vogel's smile defined the fine lines around her eyes.

She was a puzzlement of contradictions. Those fine lines signified a certain amount of maturity, yet her hair remained untouched by gray.

"Thank you, Ms. Vogel."

The final read-through of the contract was swift, and

Kyzel used the Earth-style writing implement—a *pen*—to sign. Then he slid the sheaves back across the desk.

She smiled up at him from her chair. "That's it. Now, before I distract you with your match's name and profile, and the all-important picture, allow me to introduce you to your telephone." She picked up the human-palm-sized rectangular device on her desk and offered it to him. "It's your way to communicate while on Earth. You can use it to talk to me, your date, and anyone else whose number you get. I'll show you how to use it before you leave and have you make a few practice calls to me."

"I… You are too kind," And he was a simpleton for not having thought of this himself. Rol and Fyad would be easy to reach through his wrist implant, but the people of this planet had different technology.

"Also," Ms. Vogel continued. "I already sent your date's files to your phone for you to view. I'll send her your files in a moment. You can call her tonight. The earlier the better. Calling late upsets some people. Now, let's get you trained to use this thing."

It took one quarter of an Earth hour before Kyzel mastered the basics of the *phone*. Then Ms. Vogel showed him how to access his date's file. The face that appeared on the screen was of a female close in age to himself, and his breath hitched in his chest. She had straight hair—*blonde*, according to her file.

So, blonde was pale hair with silver strands mixed in. He squinted. The file said her eyes were blue, but they could pass for gray. It was difficult to tell, as she had covered them with a black-framed vision device that perched on the bridge of her long, straight nose.

But her smile; it was glorious, the way it stretched across her face and pushed her cheeks up.

"So?" Ms. Vogel's question drew his attention away from the angel on the phone screen. She had propped her elbows on the glass-covered wooden surface of her desk and rested her chin on her fists. "What do you think of Ms. Robyn Martin Donahue?"

"I...I...." He returned his gaze to the phone. "She is *beautiful*."

This was already going better than he had expected.

"Good," Ms. Vogel replied. "Adam, my assistant, will take you back to your suite so you can review the rest of her file before you set up a meeting. Tomorrow is Friday, and she doesn't work, so you might arrange to meet her during the day. *If* she doesn't already have plans."

"Very well. Thank you, Ms. Vogel. I will *call* you if I have any other questions." He turned his attention to Rol. "Are you ready to go?"

"I am."

Ms. Vogel led them back out to the lobby, and her assistant, Adam took over. The *elevator*, as Adam called the moving box room, took them to the top floor of the five-story building. It was tight inside, with the three Bezchians holding their wings close so Adam could slip in next to the numbered buttons.

The small human male pressed the button marked *5*, then smiled at them. "Five is your floor. The button above, marked *R*, is for the roof. You may use the roof to come and go. It'll probably be easier than going all the way down to the first floor and using the doors."

The sensation of the box smoothly rising only lasted a moment before the doors opened again onto a wide, well-lit corridor.

So, an elevator is a lift between the floors. Very similar to the platforms the Galactic Alliance used at their facilities. At home, ramps within a structure served the same purpose.

Adam stepped out of the elevator and beckoned them to follow him. "Your prints are in the system, so just press any finger to a scanner and the doors will open for you."

A pleasant, mellow scent teased Kyzel's nose. "What is that smell?"

Adam sniffed the air. "That is vanilla. We have a rotation of air fresheners we use, but if you don't like it, I can have them turned off."

"No. I like this one." Kyzel inhaled again. "It is quite agreeable. Can we get it in our accommodations?"

"Sure. I'll take care of it." Adam stopped in front of a silvery-green pair of doors, and pressed his finger to a black circle set in the cream-colored wall. A green light glowed around the edge of the button and the doors slid open with a pleasant sigh. "This is your suite. Go on in and make yourselves comfortable."

Kyzel stepped into the room beyond. "Spacious."

Plenty of room for them to stretch their wings without running into one another. And the furniture was compatible with Bezchian physical requirements. A long, backless, cushioned bench, three straddle-perches with forearm leaners, and a chest-high table surrounded by four tall single-seat perches. And the faint scent of vanilla.

Adam followed Rol and Fyad in, and stopped just inside the door. "This is the common area. There's a kitchen through the archway to your right, and a study behind those doors on the left. Through that center archway are four sleeping areas. Each room has its own toilet and bath facilities. Dinner is served in the dining hall on the first floor, starting in about an hour. If you decide to cook here, send me a grocery list of what you need twenty-four hours in advance. Every effort will be made to find suitable replacements for anything unavailable on Earth. Any questions?"

"I have none." Kyzel glanced at Rol. Fyad was already down the hall, presumably securing the sleeping rooms.

Rol shook his head. "I have no questions."

"Well, then." Adam seemed satisfied. "Have a great evening."

"Thank you, Adam." Kyzel gave the Earthling male a nod, and Adam retreated, heading back in the direction of the elevator.

"All clear, my monarch."

Kyzel turned his attention to his bodyguard, now standing at the entrance to the sleeping accommodations. "Thank you, Fyad."

Rol waved his hand in the direction of the luggage at Fyad's feet. "Kind of them to bring in our bags. Shall we unpack, then go down for dinner?"

"You may." Kyzel turned toward the entrance to the travelers' nest—or suite, as Adam had called it. "I am going to go see Ms. Donahue now."

"I will go with you, then."

That was what he had feared Rol would say. "No." He raised one hand. "I go to meet her alone."

Rol ruffled his wings, his agitation clear. "You cannot go alone. You are our monarch."

Fyad nodded his black-feathered head. "It would be unwise for you to go alone on a strange planet."

He spared a glance over Rol's shoulder at Fyad. "No one knows I am here yet, there will be no danger. If all three of us show up at her nest, it may upset her."

"But...." Rol spluttered.

"You are *not* going with me to meet my mate, Rol. I will inform you how it goes. You can unpack your baggage while you wait."

FOUR

Robyn gave the front door a gentle shove closed with her foot. *Ah. Home, sweet home.*

Time enough for a quick bath before she walked over to Meryl's house, a block away. She dropped her purse on the sofa and carried the mail into the kitchen.

"Bill…bill…real estate postcard… junk… magazine renewal…" Why did she still bother getting the home decorating magazine? *Because I like the tactile experience.* "…junk…junk—"

The rap of knuckles against her front door drew a groan from deep inside. *Guess Kevin wasn't finished talking. Once an idiot….*

No, no, no. She'd sworn she'd never treat anyone the way Kevin had treated her, and that promise had included Kevin. But that didn't mean she couldn't give him a piece of her mind.

She stomped toward the door, grasped the knob, and yanked the door open. "*Why*, Kevin? Why can't you just…? *Ohh.*"

Man-nipples. She was looking at man-nipples, not Kevin's face. How…unexpected.

A vaguely nutmeggy scent floated on the subtle evening breeze as she tipped her head back, and back, and back. Her gaze roved over the leather straps across a smooth, bare chest, until she met the piercing ice-blue gaze of her rather enormous…and ridiculously handsome…visitor. The guy had to be pushing seven feet; too tall to pass through her doorway without ducking.

And his hair—which wasn't really hair, but more like fine, sleeked-back feathers—ran over his head from a low widow's peak back. A lot like a bald eagle, but with more silver and gray than white.

"Good evening, Ms. Donahue." Her ridiculously handsome visitor had a ridiculously deep and sexy voice. The kind of voice that reached out and caressed her in all the places she hadn't been caressed in, well, way too long. And never properly.

A subtle motion drew her attention to something big, silvery-white, and feathery behind his broad shoulders.

Her breath hitched in her chest. "*OhdearGod!*"

She slammed the door shut, the bang cracking through the quiet of the house.

Breathe, Robbi. Breathe.

But the guy has wings!

Honest-to-God wings. What was she supposed to do with this?

Help…she needed help. *Meryl*. Yes, Meryl would know what to do.

She rushed to the sofa, grabbed her purse, and hurried into the dining room. The safest place during an earthquake was under a table. This wasn't an earthquake, but her proverbial foundation had been shaken, so under the table was as good as any place to hide. Because God only knew if the guy was peeking through her windows right now.

I'm not paranoid. I'm not paranoid.

Once under the piece of sturdy oak furniture, she dug her hands into her purse, fumbling for her phone. Where…*there*. She closed her hand around the piece of hard plastic and drew out the device.

Several call and text alerts popped up on the screen. *Darn you, Kevin.*

Her hands trembled with the shock of adrenaline blasting through her.

"Focus, girl. Forget the texts. Push *Recents*…good. And there's Meryl." She stabbed at her friend's number and raised the phone to her ear.

"Hey, chick-a-roo." Meryl's cheery voice failed to induce the calm Robyn so desperately needed. "Are we still wining tonight? Kit-Kat is here."

My daughter is there? That was good. She needed numbers, a show of force. "Meryl." The hoarse whisper didn't even sound like her voice. "There's a thirty-foot man at my front door."

"A thirty-foot…. Ohh, hon-*neeeey*."

"Stop it."

"Stop what?"

"Stop thinking about the size of his…his…his…."

"His dick?"

"Auntie!" Kathy's shocked voice carried over the receiver.

It was all for show, of course. No one could have Meryl as a godmother and not have learned a thing or two about dirty words.

"His…penis." Robyn forced the word through her teeth. Only Meryl could one-track a conversation so fast. "This is serious."

"So am I." Meryl sounded more gleeful than serious.

"Okay. Okay, fine. He's not *actually* thirty-feet, but he is taller than my front door."

"Shit, Robyn, what are you waiting for? Drag him inside!"

"No, *no*, stop it. Meryl, he has *wings*." Beautiful silver-gray wings.

Her fingers twitched at the thought of their softness— because they would be soft, of course.

"You're not talking about buffalo wings for dinner, are you?"

"No. Humongous, real-life, wings." She gave her free hand a wave, for no apparent reason since no one was there to see it. "Sprouting from his back."

"Leathery, or feathery?"

"Feathery, like an angel's." More like a bird of prey's really. A larger-than-life bird of prey's.

"So, there's an 'angel' at your front door." It was a statement, not a question.

"Yes." A wild thought popped into her mind. She cupped her hand over the speaker and her mouth. "Like Lucifer."

"You mean the guy from the T.V. show?"

"*No*. He's at least thirty years older than that." And better looking in a seasoned sort of way. *Steady, Robbi.* "Meryl, what if it *is* Lucifer?"

Meryl's burst of laughter came from the itty-bitty phone speaker. Great. But in all fairness, the thought had sounded more plausible in her head. Once put into words, it sounded crazy. *She* sounded crazy.

"What's going on, Auntie?"

"Sh, Kit-Kat. Wait a minute. Robyn?"

"I'm still here." *Still need help.*

"That makes no sense. You've led the most squeaky-clean life imaginable. If Lucifer was going to show up on *anyone's* doorstep, it'd be mine before it'd be yours, don'tcha think?"

She had a point. "Probably."

"You know that's true, Ms. I-Don't-Cuss." Meryl sighed. "Listen, could he be your off-world match from Silverstar?"

The sensation of puzzle pieces clicking into place in her brain was almost audible. "W-wouldn't they have called or texted me first?"

"Maybe they sent him as a surprise?"

"Do they do that?"

Meryl made a small laugh sound. "I don't know, honey. Why don't you ask the *angel* on your doorstep?"

Well, duh. Why didn't she think of that?

Because you're a crazy old lady. The only thing missing were cats, and that was because she was allergic.

"Fine. Okay. I will."

"Good! Now go get him before he leaves. And don't worry about calling me back if you get it on with him."

"Meryl—"

"*Ciao*, Robbi. Have fun."

The beep of her friend disconnecting ended the call, and she stared at her phone's screen.

Oh, for goodness sake. Somewhere in the middle of the seventeen texts and calls from Kevin, Nixy Vogel from Silverstar *had* texted her. Yes, her match had been made, and his bio was attached. Yes, he had arrived on Earth already, and would contact her once he was settled into his suite. No, Robyn was under no obligation to agree to a date unless she was comfortable with doing so.

There was even a head shot of the guy—Kyzel Raptorclaw from Bezchi. His home world was a long-time member of the Galactic Alliance of Planets, and they'd just begun working on a trade treaty with Earth—in Los Angeles of all places, a short trip down the freeway distance-wise.

She pushed her glasses up higher on her nose and peered through the magnification lenses. Yep, a bit of his feathery wings showed behind his head. And the widow's peak just added to his general gorgeousness, that was for darn sure.

And I left all that *standing on my front porch, visible to every last single woman in the neighborhood?*

She scrambled out from under her dining table, gave her blouse a tug to make sure it was straight, and hurried her hiney in the direction of her front door. Hopefully slamming the door in his face wasn't an insult on his planet.

Here goes nothing.

Or everything. Her heart gave a mad flutter of giddy anticipation. The sense that her life was about to completely and irrevocably change settled over her. She grasped the doorknob, turned, and pulled the door open…

…to an empty porch.

No one—alien nor angel—stood there.

She leaned forward and peered left and right. Nope. The porch was devoid of life, as was the front walk and the sidewalk.

"Well, that's disappointing." She allowed her shoulders to slump.

Apparently the winged off-worlder only knocked once, and she'd blown it. Once again, she'd sabotaged her love life without even trying.

A warm puff of air stirred the stillness of the evening, and something floated across her porch. She bent and pinched the delicate silver feather between her thumb and forefinger. It was beautiful, ethereal, like the glow of a full moon in the darkest night.

She brought it to her nose and inhaled. A comfortable, nutmeggy scent filled her with an odd sense of rightness.

"Kyzel." Her whisper seemed to surround her.

I need to text Nixy Vogel and tell her what happened.

Nixy could get a message to Kyzel. Hopefully he'd understand she hadn't intentionally jilted him, and would agree to meet her somewhere. A special place he'd find interesting. But where? She didn't know anything about him or what he liked.

Read his bio in the text, dummy.

All might not be lost after all. She clutched the feather to her breast, stepped back inside, and closed the door. First things first. Text Nixy, then get to know Kyzel as well as a bio would allow.

The rest would come.

FIVE

For one beautiful and breathless moment, an angel had stood in the doorway of Robyn Martin Donahue's tiny nest.

House.

Home.

He must remember the correct words in her language.

Ah, but she was more stunning in reality than in her photograph. Her pale, straight hair parted just off center and swept down to brush her shoulders. And her eyes, as blue as Lake Tic'va, peering out through the dark-framed vision enhancers.

Glasses. They are called glasses.

And her scent; it was like the vanilla air freshener from the suite, only subtler, softer. Between that and her curvy form, he was transfixed as his blood turned molten in his veins. Careene had been small by raptor standards, but Robyn Donahue barely reached mid-chest. The urge to pull her close and wrap her in the protective circle of his wings nearly overrode his common sense. Somehow, he had managed to remember enough to greet her by her formal name, as was proper.

Then, she slammed the door—the resounding bang had echoed across the front lawn—leaving him alone on the narrow porch. An unexpected development, to be sure.

"It appears your venture has failed, my friend."

The sound of Rol's voice behind him intruded, along with the curious creak-buzz sound of some sort of Earth insect in the bushes.

Kyzel turned partway and glared at his friend. "Have you already finished unpacking?"

Rol stood on the front path and shrugged. "I cannot deny my own curiosity. I must say, the human female's reaction disappointed me."

"Fortunately, I do not consider this venture a failure based on the outcome of one meeting."

It was a shame he had failed to foresee Robyn's reaction. Even on Bezchi, it was not good if a female screamed and slammed her door, leaving a male standing on the doorstep.

"An outcome that concerns me. Our second monarch must be as strong as our first. She cannot run and hide at the first sign of adversity."

"She was not expecting me, therefore reacted appropriately." The need to defend Robyn Martin Donahue was like a rod straightening his spine. "I will not give up on her."

What had he done wrong? Had he offended her? If so, how? Maybe it was too late for him to visit?

"Knocking again would be rude," Rol said. "Come off the porch before you knock something over."

He let his gaze roam the porch. There was just enough room for the two white wooden slat chairs and tiny matching table off to one side, and a long, swinging perch chair on the other. But it was the host of pots filled with lush plants that decorated the porch floor, steps, and rails that were in the most danger of accidental breakage. And the destruction of his potential mate's property would not endear him to her. He backed off the porch, one step at a time.

Once he was clear, he turned to face Rol. "I must speak with Ms. Vogel tonight."

"It is too late. She has left for the day. I saw her walk out of the building as I flew after you." Rol gestured toward the street with one hand. "Since it is already too dark to risk flying in this unfamiliar place, we can walk back to the travelers' nest together."

The humans would undoubtably gawk at them, but walking was the safer option. "I welcome your company back to our *suite*."

Rol rolled his eyes but said nothing about the correction, so Kyzel fell in step with his friend.

Since Ms. Vogel had gone home for the night, it was on him to devise a plan to properly introduce himself to Robyn Martin Donahue. But how? And when? If it was too late to call her now, was there an appropriate time to do so tomorrow?

He glanced at Rol's stoic profile. "Do you think it would be better to use the phone, or return to her house in person?"

"I think it would be wiser to return home. You, however, will naturally disagree."

"Rol...."

"I know, I know." His friend shook his head. "Believe it or not, I would be disappointed if you gave up so easily."

Not enough to dispute that choice, certainly. "I will see this through."

He must. The wave of mind-altering rightness that had taken him when she had appeared in the doorway was something he wanted to experience again.

"It boggles my mind that you are actually asking *me* for advice on females."

They rounded the corner onto the street the agency was located on. Several delicious scents drifted from the plethora of restaurants that lined both sides of the street, bombarding his olfactory senses. Based on the increased numbers of humans occupying *sidewalk* space, it was safe to say this was a favorite dining area.

"You have had your share of consorts during your life. There must be some wisdom you can share with me." It was not easy to ignore the Earthling's stares, although it was amusing how most of the humans gave them a wide berth.

Rol chuckled, but did not respond.

There was no need to push for an answer either, as they had five more blocks to walk. When the city was built, the founders had wisely laid it out on a grid of straight streets. It made navigation easier—both on foot and in the air. Although, those same founders probably had had no idea anyone would someday be able to fly above their city.

How would they have reacted to meeting a raptor like him?

"What are they doing?" Rol muttered. "The couple across the street."

Kyzel gave the male and female a surreptitious sideways glance. The female had her phone raised in his direction. It was a position that suggested she was taking photographs, as Ms. Vogel had taught him earlier this afternoon.

"Did you bring Fyad?"

Rol grunted. "I told him to stay at the travelers' nest in case you came back."

"Why do you suppose the female is taking photographs of us?"

"Because of our glorious wings?"

Kyzel met his friend's gaze and raised his eyebrows.

"Excuse me?" A female on their side of the street dragged his attention away from Rol.

This one was alone, and dressed mostly in black. Black pleated skirt, black net-like leg coverings, heavy, thick-soled black boots, black bag slung over her shoulder. Even her earlobe-length hair and eyeliner were black. The only things not entirely black were her red and black-checked shirt and her lip coloring, which was so dark a red it may as well have been black. All of that made her pale skin tone seem stark.

She stood, fist on her hip and her head cocked to one side, staring at them as if they were a puzzle to solve. "Are ya guys lost?"

Was that a tiny gemstone in her nostril?

Kyzel shook his head. "No, we are not."

"Okay." She nodded. "It's just that the only off-worlders we see around here are usually lost...or staying at the Silverstar suites. That's it, isn't it? You're Silverstar clients."

His nape feathers ruffled as a quiver of unease ran up his spine. "We are not lost. Thank you for your concern."

38

He strode forward, and the youngling stepped out of his path. Rol's footsteps sounded close behind. "Do not look back, Rol."

"I will not," his friend murmured.

Something about the female did not ring true. Not in a foreboding way, just not quite right. He turned his head a fraction to one side, but there was no sound of footsteps in pursuit.

A block away from the Silverstar building, he slowed his pace. The streets here were almost empty of humans, most likely due to the lack of restaurants. "You have not answered my question, and I am open to any knowledge you can impart about wooing a female."

Rol's burst of laughter bounced off the buildings. "Find something she likes, then present it to her."

Of course. How had he not thought of that? Her bio would contain every bit of information he could possibly need. He would memorize it tonight, and tomorrow he would call on Robyn Martin Donahue again.

With luck, she would be more receptive.

SIX

Robyn sat in one of the white Adirondack rocking chairs on her front porch. Birdsong in the trees glorified the joy of living, and the cool morning air held a promise of warmer temperatures to come later in the afternoon.

In other words, a typical late-summer day in southern California.

She raised her steaming mug and inhaled the deep, rich cinnamon aroma of her favorite blend of Kona coffee. Mornings like this, especially when such mornings fell on a Friday, were the best. No work, no obligations, just her and nature, and....

Meryl rounded the end of the neighbor's hedge, her tightly curled mop of bleached golden hair bouncing. She strode up Robyn's front path with a confidence borne from having faced life's hard knocks and survived.

Her friend spread her arms wide as she ascended the two steps to the porch. "I cannot tell you how disappointed I am to see you out here this morning, alone. Where *is* he?"

"*He* is not here." She set her mug on the whitewashed wood table between the chairs.

"Obviously." Meryl plopped herself in the second rocker. "I'd so hoped you had an overnight house guest. Are those your aunt's cinnamon rolls I smell?"

"Yep. They're in the oven." Robyn picked up the white carafe and tipped it to fill the waiting mug. The soft sound of bird wings swooshed past the porch. "Why would you come over if you thought he'd spent the night?"

"I figured I'd walk by to see." Meryl accepted the now-full mug. "And there you were, fully dressed and sitting on your porch. If he was here, you wouldn't be dressed...or on the porch, if you know what I mean."

A snort escaped Robyn. Yeah, she knew all right. "Sorry to disappoint you."

"Sorry that you're disappointed, and probably don't realize it." Meryl's grin was full of innuendo. "So, you ready to talk?"

"There's nothing to talk about." She blew out a short, heavy breath. "By the time I hung up with you and got back to the door, he was gone."

Except for that feather. There was something about it. It had called to her from her vanity last night as she'd tossed and turned in bed. Until she'd finally caved in after forty-five minutes and relocated it to her pillow. It was weird how the combination of the downy soft piece of fluff and the scent of nutmeg, was all it took to zonk her out.

And the dreams she'd had...oh, boy. Or, "whoa" boy. Her gaze was drawn to the buzz of a hummingbird flitting around the feeder at the other end of the porch. She'd never had such sexually charged dreams, even back in the days when she believed Kevin was her one-and-only.

"Was he from the Silverstar Agency?"

Robyn blinked away the lovely wisps of her dreams and refocused on her friend. "Actually, yes. You were right, Nixy had texted me. Unfortunately, it was during a barrage of Kevin texts that I was ignoring, so I missed it."

"That bastard. You'd think that, after five years, he'd get the hint." Meryl took another sip from her mug. "He *is* denser than most."

A snicker escaped Robyn. She couldn't disagree with that observation.

"Anyhoo," Meryl continued. "What are you going to do about your angel?"

The chime of the timer on her phone going off filled the space with its happy tune. The hummingbird gave an alarmed chirp and darted away. "I'm going to get breakfast out of the oven."

"Not what I meant, but I'm too hungry to argue." Meryl trailed her into the house like a shadow.

Minutes later, the cinnamon rolls were cooling on a rack and more coffee was brewing. Robyn set two forks and napkins on the breakfast bar, then leaned back against the sink as Meryl retrieved a couple of plates. Being in the same neighborhood of small 1930s craftsman bungalows, and in houses with the same floorplan, had its advantages.

The plates clinked together as Meryl set them on the bar. "You going to answer my question?"

"Well, I texted Nixy Vogel last night to explain the situation, and asked how to fix it." She gave her shoulders a shrug. "I guess she'll text back once she gets into the office."

"Probably...." Meryl's gaze flitted to somewhere over her shoulder. "Ohh."

"Oh, what?"

"It looks like *someone* got that text."

"What?" She turned to look out the kitchen window, and the massive male figure striding up her front path. It was *him*...Kyzel Raptorclaw. *"Ohh."*

His tan skin held the lovely warmth of golden honey. And, oh my, the silver in his variegated wing feathers practically glowed in the sunlight. Was it possible for him to seem even larger and more ridiculously magnificent this morning than he had last evening—even though his man-nipples were now covered with a drapey, sky-blue shirt thingy?

The answer was, yes. Yes, it was.

"Aw, he even has flowers," Meryl breathed out. "Yellow tulips, your favorite."

Robyn glanced at the bright bouquet held to his chest in one large hand. How had he known those were her favorite?

Because you included that in your application, you dolt.

A sudden flurry of motion drew her attention back to Meryl. Her friend had sprung into action as if poked by a cattle prod.

Robyn frowned. "What are you doing?"

"Leaving." Meryl tore a paper towel from the roll and wrapped it around two cinnamon rolls.

"But, why?"

Her friend's expression turned incredulous. "Honey, do you *see* what's walking onto your porch right now?"

Well, yeah, she kinda had. The entire neighborhood probably had, too.

"That's all yours, and you don't need me around to interfere." Meryl winked. "Call me later. Have fun."

Then she was gone, the back door closing with a sharp *snick* before Robyn could think up another protest.

Kyzel drew his wings in close to his back and stepped onto Robyn Martin Donahue's small front porch. Today would be different than last night. This time, when she opened her door, she would find him "presentable."

He smoothed his free hand over his omlek. According to Ms. Vogel's early morning text, wearing a torso covering would make him less intimidating than his standard flying leathers. Apparently, Earthling males did not make a habit of showing up shirtless for their first meeting with a female. Not in this locale, at any rate. The Bezchian style shirt covered his chest and back, yet allowed his wings free range of motion.

The flowers—yellow *two-lips*, per Robyn's bio—bobbed cheerily with each step. He frowned at the bouquet. How odd that, despite their name, they looked nothing like one lip, let alone two. More like dainty cups. But these were supposedly her flower of preference, and he was determined to make a better impression this morning.

A delicious scent that smelled like the sacred spice cinbin wafted through the open doorway. He gave his wings a shake, lifted his hand, rapped his knuckles against the doorframe three times in quick succession, then took a small step back.

"Be right there." Her voice, like a melody, drifted to him from inside the house.

The quick slap-slap of her footsteps approached the door, and then, she was there. Her bright blue gaze met his, and her smile was welcoming. "Hi."

"Hello, Robyn Martin Donahue. I am Kyzel Raptorclaw. The Silverstar Agency matched us."

"I know, now." She pushed her silver-blonde hair back over one ear. "I read your bio. You can just call me Robyn. I'm really sorry about slamming the door in your face last night. I didn't realize who you were."

"It is understandable. I have since discovered that it is proper for me to contact you first instead of coming over unannounced." He extended his arm, presenting her with the *two-lips*. "And to bring a 'courting gift.'"

"Oh, my favorite." A faint pink color dusted her cheeks as she accepted his gift.

The brush of her fingers against his sent the heat of a thousand suns through his veins and into his crotch. He stifled his gasp even as she took in a sharp breath. Had she felt it too?

He cleared his throat and managed to give her a teasing grin like nothing had happened. "I, uh, know. I also read your bio."

Her laugh folded around him as she brought the flowers to her breasts. "Thank you. Would you like to come in?"

"I would." He eyed the doorway. "Most of Earth's doorways are not built with Bezchians in mind, however, I have been working on a technique." He shifted his shoulders, drew his wings together, then pulled them against his back.

"If you would step back, please."

"Sure." She retreated inside several steps.

This had all the wingmarks of an awkward situation, but he was committed now. He turned his body sideways and hugged one side of the door frame. One wing and leg in first, duck his head, twist, and…in.

"Bravo." Robyn laughed again, a delightful sound he would never tire of hearing. "I wasn't sure how you were going to do that, but it worked."

He folded his wings as close to his back as possible. "I will try not to knock anything over."

"I trust you." She moved to stand next to the tall counter between the front room and what was clearly her food preparation area. "Are you hungry?"

He inhaled deeply through his nose; the aroma of cinbin was much stronger here. "I have not eaten yet this morning. What is this delicious scent?"

"My aunt's cinnamon rolls. Old family recipe. Reminds me of her every time I make them." She rounded the end of the counter, waving her hand in the direction of the four backless perches. "Pick any stool you want while I fix you a plate."

"*Cinnamon.* Is that what I smell?" He slid onto one of the middle perches…stools…to give his wings room to relax. "It smells similar to a spice on my planet called cinbin."

"Oh, that's cool." She turned on the faucet and water flowed into a white vase. "Cooking with cinnamon reminds me of Christmas. I love it."

"You *cook* with this spice?"

"Yeah." She placed the *two-lips* in the vase and set them

on the counter. "And I'd be happy to try your *cinbin* in a recipe if you'd like…. Aaaand the expression on your face tells me I just said something wrong."

He opened and closed his mouth, then rubbed his hand over his face. "Please forgive me. On Bezchi, cinbin is a sacred spice used only by the Firewing clan during re…during a certain ritual. The thought of cooking with it seems…unusual."

"Ah. I can see why. Sorry if I was insulting in any way." The way she leaned against the other side of the counter, worrying her bottom lip between her teeth, was endearing.

"Not at all. I am sure there are many new things we will be learning as we get to know each other." Like why he could still smell her vanilla scent over the cinnamon?

Her smile brightened and she gathered up the two plates sitting on the counter. "I'd like that a lot. So—" She scooped up a fist-sized roll, glistening gooey reddish-brown threads dripping under the spatula. "—it's pronounced Bez-chee then, right?"

"That is correct."

"Good." The roll slid onto the plate and she placed it in front of him. "I was nervous that I might pronounce it wrong."

"I appreciate your attentiveness. Thank you." He could not seem to focus anywhere else except on her.

Everything about her appealed to him, right down to the way she sucked the sticky concoction off her thumb as she came back around the end of the counter.

She slid onto the stool next to his and smiled up at him. "Bon appetit."

His translator chip made a fizzle sound, then spat out, "Well hunger."

He frowned. "I do not understand."

"What, bon appetit? It's French for enjoy your food."

"Ah." He tapped his finger behind his ear where the implant rested just under his skin. "My translator is programed for English only. Maybe I should expand to include other Earth languages."

"Hmm. Well, maybe Spanish too, but otherwise don't worry. I don't mind helping out when you're stumped." She turned her attention to her roll. "So. Besides most of the doors being too small, and English being a complicated mishmash of other languages, what do you think of Earth so far?"

He waited until she raised her beautiful blue gaze back to his, then smiled. She stopped chewing her food. "Earth is quite arresting."

SEVEN

---◆---

Rol tucked his wings in and peered around the end of the hedge between Kyzel's match's nest and her neighbor's. His friend seemed elated as he had closed the distance between the sidewalk and the front door, the yellow flowers in hand. Who had ever heard of giving dying flora to win a female's attention? It would not work, of course. Even the Earthling in question would find the gesture silly.

At least, that was what part of him hoped—that Kyzel would see the folly of his actions and they could return home, where they belonged. Observe the traditions their people had adhered to for thousands of sun migrations. In other words, be normal and not anger the elders of the Firewing clan. Or any of the other clans.

Yet, Kyzel would take failure hard. His friend's heartache would also be his. It was a predicament, to be sure.

A furtive movement at the corner of the house drew his attention. What was this? Another human female, sneaking around from the back of the nest? He narrowed his eyes at the interloper. Could she be a threat to his monarch?

The female pressed her slim, long-limbed body against the side of the nest and tilted her head to one side, clearly eavesdropping on the verbal interchange between Kyzel and the female on the porch. The morning sun brought out the rich, velvety brown of her skin, and her curly hair glowed gold. A low growl rumbled in his throat, and his fingers twitched as if eager to touch her.

Rol gave himself a mental shake. This response was wholly unacceptable. Even though the new Earth female did not appear to be armed, it was best to keep his thoughts clear and focused, just in case she was a security risk. Fyad was somewhere nearby, watching out for their monarch, but the royal guard might not be close enough to stop the female if she charged up onto the porch and attempted to inflict harm.

On the other wing, if she was not intent upon causing havoc, she would most likely circumvent the hedge to pass into the neighboring yard without being seen.

He quirked one corner of his mouth up. Either way, he would be there to intercept her.

Meryl clutched the paper towel-wrapped cinnamon rolls to her chest and peeked around the corner of Robyn's house. Drat, the hot off-worlder hadn't gone inside yet…no, wait, he was trying to fit through the doorway without leaving his wings on the porch.

She swallowed down the rising snicker of amusement. Silverstar had given Robyn one helluva gift to get through her front door.

Wonder if he has a brother?

Didn't she wish? She huffed a tiny laugh. The coast was clear now, and it was time to head home. She pulled out her phone as she squeezed between Robyn's rhododendron bush and the neighbor's eight-foot hedge. A text from her goddaughter and one from an email advertiser. Nothing from Silverstar. Bummer.

Maybe they were working on something better for her in the date-a-hot-off-worlder department. She shoved the phone into the back pocket of her white denim shorts, and her nose twitched at the intrusion of a new scent. Had Robyn added a dash of allspice to her Aunt Ava's rolls this time—"*Oomph.*"

She stumbled backward a step. What the hell had she run into? A tree? She raised her gaze up, and up some more.

Not a tree…a man…off-worlder…. Tall, but not quite as tall as Robyn's new guy. Maybe six and a half feet, give or take. And, wonder of wonders, he also had *wings*. Mottled brown streaked with gray. Must be another Bezchian, with the most striking eye colors. One gray and one blue. Goddamn, that was sexier than sin.

Well, sexier than sin if he weren't glowering down at her like he might eat her up. And didn't that sound like fun?

"What are you doing?" The deep, gravelly timbre of his voice sent a shiver from the top of her head all the way down to the ends of her toes—and everywhere in between.

All she could do was stare up at him and pray he'd speak again, because she would flat out orgasm if he did.

Wait…he wanted to know what *she* was doing? She had more reason to be here than he did. This was her best friend's house.

"Going home." Her voice sounded pithy even to her. "What are *you* doing?"

He screwed up his face in an affronted manner. "I am Kyzel's adv...friend."

"You mean the big guy with wings that just went into my best friend's house?"

"Yes."

Well, not a brother per se, but close enough. Things were looking up.

She extended her free hand. "I'm Meryl Faulkner."

He stared at her hand like it was a worm. Or more like how *she'd* stare at a worm. Could be hawks thought quite highly of worms. She'd never really paid attention before.

He jutted his chin in the direction of her appendage. "What is this you are doing with your hand?"

"Offering to shake hands with you." *Duh.*

"But, *why?*" He shook his head, his confusion evident.

Aw, Meryl, cut the guy a little slack. "It's a way of greeting another person around here."

His frown deepened. "Show me."

"Please."

"What?"

Someone hadn't been paying attention when the Earth etiquette manual was handed out. "It's polite to say please when you ask someone to do something for you."

"I see." He stuck out his left hand. "Show me, please."

"Not that hand." This was like teaching a child. "The other hand."

He switched hands. The expectation that she'd follow through showed in his stance.

She slid her palm against his and wrapped her fingers around his hand. Sort of. His hand was nearly twice as large as hers, though, as a tall woman, her hands weren't puny. And, sweet Jesus, what was happening to her? It was like a hot coal was trapped between their palms, sending an invisible flame up her arm.

She released his hand almost as fast as he released hers. That was the weirdest sensation, but at least it was fading as fast as it had started.

She moved her hand behind her back and flexed her fingers. "Well, yeah. That's a handshake."

"It was…." He cleared his throat. "Interesting."

You could say that again.

"Meeting you is fortuitous, Meryl Faulkner." His tone was suddenly brusque, as though about to make a business deal.

"Oh? How so?"

"I am concerned for my friend, as I am sure you are concerned for yours."

"Well, of course. Robyn is like a sister to me."

He smiled. Not a big one, but the corners of his mouth were definitely going up. "Then you will agree that this relationship is likely not in their best interests."

Wait, what? Was this guy for real? "No, actually, I don't agree."

"Why not?"

Meryl propped her empty hand on her hip. "Did Kevin send you?"

"What is a Kevin?"

"Robyn's asshole ex. He's always trying to sabotage her

dates. And you—" She gave him a poke in the chest. "—keep your nose out of her business or I'll give you reason to regret it."

"*You* will?" He said it like he was about to outright laugh in her face.

She narrowed her eyes in the most threatening manner possible. "Don't mess with an attorney. I will take you down feather by feather, and laugh the entire time."

Technically, she was retired, but only for two years. She'd kept up with the changes in the laws—on Earth at least. Intergalactic law would require some research, but she could figure it out if necessary. *He* didn't need to know that, though.

She turned away and stomped across the neighbor's freshly mowed yard. The dew that glistened so beautifully in the lawn seemed to leap onto her canvas sneakers and soak through.

Aw, yuck. Nothing like squishing all the way home. Good thing she lived only a block away.

EIGHT

Kyzel eyed the long, tall archway. It appeared to be made from a green-toned metal, woven like entwining vines. Beneath it many passed, mostly Earth fledglings who seemed unaccountably excited. The adults accompanying the fledglings appeared less enthusiastic, and more focused on keeping their young flocks from merging with other young flocks.

He turned his gaze to the female at his side. In Robyn's eyes was a mix of pride and apprehension. Coming to this place had been her recommendation. Did she fear he would not like it?

Truthfully, he had no opinion yet, but he did have questions. "Do all these fledglings belong to one family unit?"

"No. They're from different schools, taking what we call a field trip." She nodded in the direction of a boisterous group going by. "That's like an educational excursion. They come here to learn about different birds, some which they've never seen because they only live in other parts of the world."

One little fledgling stopped to stare at him with wide dark eyes. Another behind her, also staring at him, walked right into her. Both toppled over and sprawled on the ground.

"*Annabelle.*" One of the adult females hurried over. "What have we said about staring?"

"Yeah, Annabelle," the second fledgling mocked as he scrambled back to his feet. "Haven't you ever seen an off-worlder before?"

Annabelle picked herself up and dusted herself off. "You were staring too, Ben."

The adult took them each by a hand. "Enough, you two. Let's go."

Both of the fledglings kept pace with her, craning their heads around so far to continue staring their necks must hurt. And then they were gone, melting into the crowd.

Kyzel met Robyn's gaze. "Ah."

"Yes. Ah." She grimaced. "I'm sorry."

"For what?"

"People staring." She caught her bottom lip between her teeth and shrugged. "You'd think after so many years of off-world visitors, people wouldn't do that so much."

"I do not mind. The wings are an unusual feature on most worlds. Even I recognize this." He made a sweeping gesture with his hand toward the archway. "Global Avery Sanctuary?"

Robyn's eyes widened slightly. "You can read English too?"

"It is a multi-media translator."

"Oh, neat." She grinned. "It's Aviary, not Avery."

"A-vi-ary." He gazed down at her. "A home for birds? Is this why you brought me here?"

"Uh." An attractive pink tinge dusted her cheeks, visible even through her glasses. "Not exactly...sort of. It's just that you remind me of a bird of prey—like an eagle—and I thought...." She covered her face with her hands. "Oh, my gosh, it sounds so silly now."

He moved to stand in front of her, and placed his hands on her shoulders. "Robyn."

She slipped her hands down enough to peer over her fingertips at him.

"I would be honored to view the creatures of your world that are so similar to my people."

"You would?" She lowered her hands to chin level.

"Of course."

Relief sparkled in her blue eyes and her smile was all his. "That's great. Ready, then?"

"Yes." In so many ways.

Robyn pursed her lips together. Ever since entering the aviary, Kyzel's eager expression had faded bit by bit. And now...well now he seemed to be MIA, even though she'd left him in front of the hummingbird window directly across from the restroom.

Who lost a seven-foot-tall winged alien in under three minutes? Just you, Robbi. Just you.

He had to be around here somewhere.

Two security guards ran past her, their expressions grim. Mild concern fluttered in her stomach. That couldn't be good. Kyzel didn't seem like the troublemaking type, but what did she know? She'd only just met him. She moved to follow the guards, jogging and weaving between kids and adults toward the huge exhibit cage along the back wall.

One of the larger enclosures. The one with an ever-growing crowd in front of it.

"Sir, come out of there, now." The words came from somewhere ahead.

A heavy weight sank into her stomach as she pushed through the crowd. Then she saw him. Kyzel. He was inside the cage, arguing with another security guard, and looking gloriously righteous. Something about the way he held his wings, high and partly unfurled, expressed such visual passion. Like an eagle prepared to defend his nest.

What he didn't seem to notice were the two guards she'd followed entering the cage through an access gate behind him.

Next to her, a young woman dressed in goth-black, with matching hair, fumbled with an expensive-looking camera. And she wasn't the only one. Others had their cell phones out to record the…the…the incident. Visions of videos being shared on the local evening news danced before her eyes and a long, low groan escaped her.

Expensive Camera Girl jerked her head up and narrowed her eyes. "Do you know him?"

Not really, apparently. She opened her mouth, but before she could utter a word, a long, muscular male arm reached passed her and the attached hand closed around the girl's camera, plucking it neatly from her hands.

"Hey." ECG tried to snatch back her equipment, hopping repeatedly and in vain. "Give that back."

"In due time," a deep voice responded.

Robyn turned, and tipped her neck back to get a look at the huge man at her shoulder. The guy was as tall as Kyzel, but much younger. Not a single crinkle at the corners of his black-as-night eyes, nor a hint a gray in his glossy black wings or headfeathers. What was another Bezchian doing here?

"No," ECG protested. "That's mine. Give it."

"Meet me under the archway in ten of your minutes." The black-feathered Bezchian met Robyn's gaze. "Come with me, Ms. Robyn. We must perform an extraction."

"A w-what?"

The newcomer cupped her elbow in his giant hand and guided her through the crowd toward the access gate. It seemed like the conversation was over and it was time for action.

They arrived at the gate, and Robyn folded her arms under her breasts. "Well? Now what? Are we going in too?"

Wouldn't that just boost the broadcast ratings?

"No," the stranger replied. "I will take it from here. Please stay in place."

That was interesting phrasing, but he had said please.

"Kee mohap." Black Wing's words meant nothing to her, but they did get an instant reaction from Kyzel. He whipped his head around and blinked.

Black Wing rattled off a string of words, then tipped his head in her direction. Kyzel's attention was instantly on her—and so were many of the cell phones, until one black wing curved around her. The new Bezchian had blocked her from the crowd's view. She gave him a grateful look, then turned her attention back to Kyzel.

It appeared that all the righteous indignation had drained from him, and his wings lowered into what she recognized as their resting position.

He turned his attention back to the human guards. "I apologize for my actions. I will leave now."

"Damn right you will," one of the guards replied as the other made a shooing motion at a peacock that had limped closer to check out the commotion. "Move along. We're gonna go have a word with the director."

Oh, great.

Kyzel nodded, and the entire group headed toward the gate. Once they'd exited, he moved to stand in front of her, curving his wings forward to create a sense of privacy as Black Wing stepped back.

"I am sorry, Robyn. I behaved rashly."

"Why—"

"Hey," one of the guards snapped. "Let's go, buddy."

She gazed up at Kyzel. There was something in his eyes that seemed to reach out to her, willing her to understand. And, she wanted to understand; wanted to give him the chance to explain.

All right then. She'd follow her heart…this time.

She turned to follow the guards, Kyzel close behind.

NINE

———————✦———————

Robyn stepped into the director's upstairs office. It was sparsely furnished—a desk, a credenza, two filing cabinets, and a pair of chairs arranged in front of the desk. A large dry erase board took up most of the left-hand wall. All in all, nothing spectacular, but the view was fantastic. The entire back wall was one-way glass that gave an unobstructed panorama of the main aviary building. Including the cage Kyzel had trespassed into.

"Here they are, Ms. Taylor," the guard who seemed to be in charge announced.

Ms. Taylor, aka the director of the aviary, could easily be summed up in one word: severe. From her high cheekbones and sharply defined jawline, to her intense dark eyes. Even her hair was pulled back, her tight curls tamed smooth into a bun at the nape of her neck. The only thing that might be soft about her was the deep brown of her skin tone.

This was a woman who took her job seriously, who'd probably fought hard to earn it. Which meant Kyzel's lack of judgement would have them dumped on the sidewalk outside the facility in less than five minutes. Minus a refund of their entrance fees.

Ms. Taylor eyed Kyzel with suspicion. "Thank you, Fred. Please wait outside."

Fred looked like he'd protest, but Ms. Taylor gave him a scathing glare. Then it seemed he couldn't get out of the office fast enough.

Yep. Severe. Even the employees didn't mess with her. Besides, there wasn't a lot of room in the office, even though Kyzel held his wings close to his back. Black Wing stood in the corridor frowning, with ECG's camera hanging around his neck.

The door closed with a soft thump, and silence settled into the room.

"So." Ms. Taylor's narrowed gaze was focused on them, the promise of a good dressing down in the depths of that gaze as she leaned back in her chair. "You broke at least a half dozen rules, committed as many safety violations, and created a stressful atmosphere for not only the birds in the habitat, but also my employees. Explain yourself."

Kyzel shifted, standing a little straighter. "I do not understand why."

"Why what?"

"Why are they imprisoned? They should fly free."

The director frowned. "You mean the birds?"

Ohh, so that's the problem. He didn't like the birds being caged. Which meant…. Oh, gracious. He had intended to free them.

"Yes," Kyzel confirmed. "Why are they kept here? And do not tell me it is for educational purposes."

The dawning of understanding lit Ms. Taylor's face too, and she actually smiled. It was a nice smile that softened her features a bit. "What are your names?"

Robyn took a step forward. "This is Kyzel Raptorclaw, visiting from Bezchi, and my name's Robyn Donahue. I'm really sorry we upset everyone. I thought this would be a good place for a, erm, first date."

Ms. Taylor nodded, her gaze traveling back and forth between them. "Normally, what you did would get you automatically ejected from the premises. But before I do that, it's important you understand that the Global Aviary Sanctuary *is* an educational center, and I sense here an opportunity to educate." She pushed back from her desk and stood. "Come with me. I have something to show you."

A few minutes later, Ms. Taylor led them into an unobtrusive building in the farthest corner of the facility. The scent of industrial disinfectant tickled Robyn's nose as they walked through a wide, airy room lined with observation windows. The place smelled a lot like a hospital.

Kyzel was alert, taking everything in with wide eyes, as if he might miss something. "What is this place?"

"The bird rescue medical center." Ms. Taylor guided him to a window. The room on the other side of the glass was empty, save for a young woman setting up trays with packaged surgical instruments. "This is our operating room, where injured and sick birds are brought. We deal with everything from broken wings to being shot with arrows, and worse."

Robyn squished her nose in sympathy for the unknown birds. "That's awful."

"Yes, well, there are awful people in this world." Ms. Taylor sighed. "And we haven't been able to save all the birds, but we do what we can."

Kyzel frowned. "I do not understand. Why do you keep them here?"

Ms. Taylor gave him a smile. "This is a bird rescue sanctuary, Mr. Raptorclaw. When a bird is healthy enough, it's returned to the wild. Freed. Not kept here in a cage."

"Then why are there caged birds?"

"Those are the ones who can't survive in the wild anymore."

Kyzel's expression cleared, and the corners of his mouth crept up into a small smile. "I see. You give them sanctuary."

"Exactly," Ms. Taylor said. "My gut tells me that what you did was simply a cultural misunderstanding. I'm going to cut you some slack, as long as you promise to stay out of the birds' habitats."

"That is very gracious of you, Ms. Taylor." Kyzel gave the director a bow. "I will respect your rules, you need not worry."

"Oh, I'll still worry, but my gut is rarely wrong. So, I'm going with it, *this time*." She nodded to each of them. "Please enjoy the rest of your day, and the sanctuary."

Kyzel gazed up as he passed under the sanctuary's beautiful archway. There was no denying that this was an institution of honor. He understood that now, although the air current to that enlightenment had been rough. For a time, he had feared Robyn would part ways with him over his misguided, rash actions.

Yet she had stayed, defended him, taken responsibility for her part, and, most importantly, was still at his side. She carried honor within her soul, as a monarch should. At some point he would have to tell her, but it was too soon. His agreement with Rol would be honored until the time was right.

He turned his gaze toward Robyn. The top of her head barely reached his elbow, yet she walked with the confidence of a warrior. She would be respected for that on his planet.

She glanced up and met his gaze. "Do you feel better about this place now?"

"Immensely. I still regret any embarrassment I caused you."

"It's all forgotten." She waved one fine-boned hand.

Apprehension gripped his insides. "You do not remember?"

Robyn slipped the same hand into his larger one. "That's a way of saying it's in the past and I have forgiven you."

Sweet relief. She did not have the early stages of the mindlessness. And, she was holding his hand of her own volition. The simple connection sent a flood of effervescent warmth through him, and his heart soared on currents of joy.

He wrapped his fingers around her hand as they strolled into the green zone—the *park*—surrounding the sanctuary. "Thank you. I will be more careful in the future."

"Don't." There was an earnestness to the word. "I mean, just be you, Kyzel. Don't worry about what I think. I can tell you, from personal experience, that always trying to live up to someone else's expectations does bad things to a person's self-esteem."

"Personal experience? Would you explain?"

She huffed a laugh. "I was married for thirty-five years to a man who expected me to fit his image of me. Once our youngest daughter graduated college, she moved out, and I walked out the door with her."

"You have a fledg…no, she is not a fledgling any longer, is she?"

"No." She grinned. "Kathy's a twenty-seven-year-old tech geek."

"Tech geek?"

"Computers. You'll see when you meet her, she understands it all. And I tell you, ever since the Galactic Alliance of Planets made first contact, there's so much new stuff to keep up with." Robyn pointed to a large red and yellow cart at the bend of the path. "Are you hungry?"

It had been many hours since *break-fast*. "I am."

"Great. Connie has the best sausages in the park…oh, wait. Do you eat meat?"

"Not all Bezchians do, but I am of the raptor clan, and we prefer meat."

"I should've known." She seemed intrigued by his revelation. "Come on."

He allowed her to take the lead. Soon they had their "Polish sausages" in hand, and found seating on the rim of a large fountain. He bit into the first sausage and the casing popped, flooding his mouth with a juicy, deliciousness he had no words to describe. Spicey, but not too hot. All he could do was close his eyes and chew, savoring the tangy alien flavors.

"Do you like it?" Robyn asked.

He swallowed the food down. "I have never tasted the like. It is outstanding."

She appeared incredibly pleased by this, then bit into her sausage…and he could not draw a breath. How could chewing be so mesmerizing? Then she swallowed, and her throat moved with the action, sending his thoughts in the most inappropriate direction possible.

That was, of course, the moment she turned her blue eyes on him and smiled. He should feel the stinging heat of embarrassment, but it was oddly absent. Instead, contentment filled all the aching, dark corners of his soul. Corners Careene had never touched.

Robyn cleared her throat. "So, do you have—"

A cry of frustrated anger drew his attention to a thicket of bushes several paces away. A female Earthling with short-cropped black hair stood gazing up with her hands on her hips. Hovering above the bushes was Fyad, something rectangular with a cylindrical appendage dangling by a strap from his hand.

"That guy with black wings was at the aviary," Robyn said. "Who is he?"

"I believe you would call him my bodyguard." Kyzel took another bite of Polish sausage.

She gave him a surprised look. "What do you do that you need a bodyguard?"

The black-haired woman shouted something indecipherable at Fyad and stomped her foot. The other Bezchian's laugh was clear, even though his words in reply were not.

He could not tell Robyn the full story yet, but he also would not lie. "I am the head of a large institution."

What was Fyad doing?

"You mean, like a high-profile company or something?"

"Hmmm." Now the black-haired female was jumping, trying to catch Fyad's foot and missing by the feather's width.

There was something familiar about her. She resembled the young human who had spoken to him and Rol on the street last night. Whatever was happening between her and Fyad now could not be good. He made a move to rise, but the touch of Robyn's hand on his arm stopped him.

"She was taking pictures of the incident at the aviary," Robyn explained. "He took her camera away from her there, too. I'm guessing she stalked us to the park and was hiding in the bushes, taking more shots of us eating."

Kyzel frowned. "Is this normal behavior for a human?"

"Not often." She shrugged her shoulders. "But, you're a high-profile businessman, so maybe she recognized you."

A stone of dread settled in his stomach. It would not be good to be recognized, not at this point, anyway.

Fyad flapped away with the strapped item, sending a whirlwind of leaves and dust circling around the obviously infuriated female.

Kyzel made a small grunt and returned his attention to Robyn. "If that is the case, then Fyad is doing his job. It irked me when my people insisted that I bring others with me as protection. Apparently, their counsel was sounder than I thought."

"You mean others came with you too?"

"Only my friend, Rol. He is one of those who worries over-much."

Robyn laughed. "My best friend, Meryl is the same about me sometimes."

"It is good to have friends who care."

"Yes, it is."

He popped the last bite of the Earth sausage into his mouth, and bit down. The lovely combinations of unfamiliar flavors were as strong with this bite as they had been with the first.

"I do not know what Polishes are, but they are delicious in a sausage. Can they be used in other foods?"

Robyn seemed to choke on her drink, and he gave her a firm pat on her back.

Finally, she caught her breath. "Polish is not an *ingredient*. It refers to the country this sausage came from originally. Poland. That's why they're called Polish sausages."

Heat rose to his face. "It seems I have much to learn about your world."

"At least as much as I have to learn about yours." She patted his forearm, and again anticipation raced through him. "Sounds like fun, huh?"

He met her bright blue gaze. "With you, yes."

She wrapped her hands around his and raised it up to study. "I thought so. You have talons instead of fingernails. Look." She held up her free hand.

The ends of her fingernails were covered with a smooth, pale pink coloring.

He peered closer. "Are they painted?"

69

"Yep. It's called fingernail polish."

"But, why?"

She shrugged one shoulder. "Because it makes me feel pretty."

He met her gaze. "You are beautiful, Robyn Martin Donahue."

Her entire face turned the same pink as her nails, but she smiled. "Thank you, but let's drop the Donahue, okay? No need to bring my ex into our conversations."

"Names work different here, I see." On Bezchi, everyone was identified by their clan. Raptorclaw, Firewing, Landwalker, and so on.

"Yeah. Someday I'll get around to legally dumping Donahue and just be Martin again." She lowered her gaze back to his hand. "So, how do your talons work?"

He extended them partway. "I can extend and retract them at will."

"Wow, that's pretty nifty. Do you use them often?"

"No." He pulled them back in so they would not scratch her. "Our kind used to hunt, but modern technology has removed that need."

"Same for most humans." She wove her fingers through his, her soft sigh full of contentment. "This has been fun, Kyzel. I'm glad you came back this morning."

So was he. "I have had a wonderful time, Robyn. Would you consider accompanying me to dinner tonight?"

Her smile lit the space between them like the sun coming out from behind a cloud. "I'd love to, Kyzel Raptorclaw."

TEN

Robyn pushed, and the hangers slid along the painted wooden closet rod. "Dress, skirt, or pantsuit, Meryl?"

"I got this, amateur." Meryl grabbed her arm and tugged. "Let me choose. You go do your make-up."

"Fine." Her friend usually did a better job picking appropriate outfits for any occasion anyway.

As she danced out of Meryl's way, a small giggle bubbled out—an honest-to-God giggle, like she was a college coed going on a date with the senior star quarterback. It was silly, but when had she ever felt like that about any of the guys she'd dated?

"He's taking you to Snodgrass's, right?" Meryl asked.

"Yep." Best steakhouse in town, and one of the few local restaurants with a palatial front door.

They also had a reputation for accommodating the specific physical needs of their off-world guests, like a chair without a back for Kyzel's wings.

"Good choice. All right, let's see here…." Meryl's words

became indecipherable mumbles as the scrape of plastic on wood resumed.

Robyn planted her bottom in the vanity chair and stared at her reflection. There was a definite spark in her eyes that she hadn't seen for…years? Decades? Certainly not since she was an infatuated nineteen-year-old bride embarking on what was supposed to be the grandest adventure of her life.

She dipped her make-up brush into the foundation and made dots across her face. That adventure had fizzled quickly. By thirty, the spark had dulled to an ember of resignation. She stroked the brush over her skin, blending the foundation into a satin-smooth finish, then moved on to her blush.

In hindsight, the clues to Kevin's control issues had been there from the beginning. How many guys went dress shopping with their fiancée and chose their wedding dress for them? Why had she ever believed that him doing so was an adorable expression of his devotion?

"Ah ha." Meryl emerged from the closet holding a hanger high. "Sexy in a black pantsuit."

Ooh, yes. The crepe, waist-hugging, flare-legged outfit with a draping neckline was elegant, and yes, even a little sexy.

"It'll look perfect with red lipstick, and your white pearl earrings."

"You mean the earrings *Kevin* gave me?" She squished her face to match her uncertainty. "Don't you think that'd be like intentionally jinxing my date with Kyzel?"

"Spare me the drama, Robbi." Meryl laid the pantsuit on the bed. "Your date is what *you* make it. Besides, those pearls are karma's way of rewarding you for all the shit you put up with from that ass-clown."

Wasn't that the truth? "You always find a way to put everything into perspective."

"And speaking of perspective." Her friend sat on the end of the bed and met her gaze. "I have a really good feeling about this guy."

"Oh, you do, do you?"

"I do."

"So do I." Robyn gave her friend a gentle smile. "There's something about him that's...different. Special. Hot."

Now Meryl laughed. "In all the years we've known each other, I've never seen you shine so much."

"Oh, please." She gave a dismissive wave and turned back to the vanity.

"Do you know how many guys you've dated who got this kind of reaction out of you?" Meryl continued. "None. Zip. Zero."

Robyn met her own gaze in the mirror again. The sparkle was still there, and just the thought of Kyzel filled her heart full to bursting. And this was only their second date. "You might have a point."

"But," Meryl lowered her voice, "he's from another planet, honey. What are you going to do if things work out?"

It wasn't that she hadn't thought about that scenario, hadn't considered the implications of a long-term relationship with Kyzel. If it were just Kevin she'd be leaving behind, the decision would be a no-brainer. But she had Karen, Kev, and Kathy to think about. Could she just up and leave her kids behind, *if* things got that serious?

She shifted her gaze to Meryl's reflection. "I...don't know."

Kyzel rapped his knuckles against Robyn's front door, then gave his wings a quick shake to release some of his tension. Rol's lack of enthusiasm about his fledgling relationship with her stung. Was it too much for his friend to stir up some sort of positivity, even if just for show?

The door opened, and Robyn stunned his senses with her smile. "Hi, Kyzel."

"Robyn." It was all he could choke out. By the immortals, she was regal in her curve-hugging black outfit. "I have missed your smile."

"Oh." The lovely rosy pink color was back in her cheeks, and she looked down at her feet in their strappy black sandals.

He reached out and brushed the backs of his fingers against the soft skin of her cheek. Her warmth heated him to his core. If the only way to look upon her was to stop breathing, he would do so, gladly.

She raised her face, her blue-eyed gaze on him only. "It's only been four hours."

"It seems longer." Much longer.

"A-*hem*." An unexpected voice from behind Robyn intruded on the moment.

Robyn startled. "Oh, sorry. Kyzel, this is my best friend, Meryl."

A tall, slender female, with tightly curled golden hair covering her head, stepped into view. "Nice to meet you, Kyzel."

He dipped his head in a greeting. "The pleasure is mine, Meryl."

"Thanks. Well, I'll be going now." Meryl hugged Robyn. "Got my own plans tonight."

"You do?" Robyn gave her friend a curious look.

"Dinner with my goddaughter, of course." Meryl moved around him and down the porch steps. "Behave yourselves, kids…or not. Ta-ta."

Kyzel tilted his head to one side. "What is a goddaughter?"

"I met Meryl a year before I got pregnant with my youngest daughter, Kathy," Robyn explained as she grabbed her purse, then closed and locked her door. "She and her husband Nathan couldn't have children, but they helped me out a lot when I ended up on bedrest. I asked them to be Kathy's godparents when she was baptized."

"Bap-tized?"

"It's a religious ceremony." She took his hand and he allowed her to lead him toward her car in the driveway. Surely, she did not intend to drive to the restaurant. "The simple explanation is that they became part of our family and…oh, dear."

She stared at her car hard, then at him, and back again. "You won't fit."

"No, I will not." It was very difficult to not crack a grin.

"It's too far to walk to Snodgrass's in these shoes." The look she gave him was bleak. "I could change into my sneakers."

"No need." He moved to stand directly in front of her. "We can fly."

Her eyes went wide with comprehension. "Isn't that…dangerous?"

"Not at all." As long as he stayed high enough to not tangle with the black wires between the poles, and low enough to avoid small Earth aircraft.

"Okay." She still sounded uncertain. "How're we going to do this?"

"I will carry you." He bent, scooped her into his arms, and cradled her against his chest. "Hang on."

He unfurled his wings, took a step, then another, faster and faster, until he was running across her front yard toward the street.

Robyn snaked her arms around his neck. "Kyyyzzeellll… the streeeeeeet!"

He gave his wings a mighty pump, and leaped.

Oh, my God, we're flying*!*

Robyn squeezed her eyes shut, then opened them again. Her house, her car, her entire neighborhood, looked like a miniature toy town. "This…is…*amazing.*"

Kyzel's deep laugh rolled over her like a warm wave. "You like the view?"

"Oh, my gosh, *yes.* Everything looks so different from up here." Different even to the view from an airplane.

A wisp of her hair came loose and whipped in front of her glasses, but there was no way she was letting go of him to fix it. "Next time I'll remember to wear a scarf."

"It is good to know there will be a 'next time.'" The deep, suggestive timbre of his voice shot straight through her like an electric bolt, ending smack dab between her legs.

She turned away from one incredible view to another: the shimmering pleasure in Kyzel's eyes. His completely black eyes. Not a bit of white showed.

"What happened to your eyes?" The words were out of her mouth before common sense kicked in.

Kyzel's smile got larger, if that was even possible. "It is a lens that protects my eyes and enhances my vision as I fly. It will help me avoid obstacles."

Well, that was reassuring.

His smile faltered. "Do they bother you?"

"No." Not in the least. They were kinda sexy, really. "I like them."

What would he do if she kissed him right now? Would that distract him enough to crash? Probably should avoid that, but a kiss on the cheek should be okay. She raised her head, aiming for his cheek, until Kyzel turned his head and she met his lips. His firm, warm lips.

Her thoughts spun like a spiraling kite, then the kite caught a breeze and soared to heights she'd never expected to reach. Who knew a simple kiss—two sets of lips moving against each other—could elicit such a reaction? Without any tongue action, even?

Kyzel pulled back, just a fraction, and snared her gaze. "So, now we know." His voice was rough and sent a thrill of excitement straight down her spine. "We both are that interested in each other... and I did not crash."

A laugh bubbled out of her. "Well, thank God for the last part. And, yes, to the first. How did you know that's what I was thinking, though?"

"Your face is very expressive." He grinned back at her. "We should be careful about how severely we test my flying skills, though. This is the first time I have carried another, other than my fledglings, and that was years ago."

Heat stung her cheeks. "Am I too heavy?"

"No." There was so much sincerity behind that word. "You are perfect."

ELEVEN

---*---

"Careene and I raised six fledglings to adulthood. Four daughters and two sons."

Robyn watched Kyzel's expression over the rim of her wine glass as he ran down the attributes of each of his children, his eyes alight with love. Bragging rights were a parent's due, but Kyzel spoke of them and their individual accomplishments without taking credit for himself. And, frankly, she'd do just about anything to keep him talking. It was like his voice resonated with her down to the marrow of her bones.

And between her legs.

Kyzel smiled. "It is one of my greatest comforts to know that Careene lived to see them fly the nest before she took on with an illness and passed to The Great Aerie a sun migration ago. Which is a *year* by your calendar."

"I'm sorry." And she meant it, even though she wouldn't be sitting here with this compassionate man if the woman were still alive.

"She no longer suffers, and that brings our heirs and me

great peace."

"Heirs? Is that what they are now that they're not fledglings anymore?" And how exactly would they feel about their father hooking up with someone from another planet?

"In a manner of speaking. All Bezchians are heirs of our world."

"Ooh, that's poetic. I like it."

Kyzel's smile brightened and he reached for his wine glass. "Now, it is your turn. Tell me about your three *children*. Is that the correct word?"

"Yes, children." Her mother's heart filled to bursting. "You know about Kathy already. She lives a half hour away. My first born, Karen lives in Colorado with her husband, and is a mother herself now. Their daughter, my granddaughter, Danica is two years old. And Kevin, Jr. is single, a geologist, and currently lives in Arizona."

Kyzel frowned. "Your former mate's name is Kevin, correct?"

Boy, he picked up on that really fast. "Yep. Remember how I said he was controlling?" She paused for him to nod. "When I was pregnant with our first baby, he wanted a boy so bad just to name it after himself. But, when we found out it was a girl, he decided her name should at least begin with a *K* like his. Did the same with Kathy."

Which wasn't even short for Kathleen or Kathrine. Just Kathy.

"Naming a fled...*child* after one's self...." He stopped. "I am sorry. It is none of my concern."

She gave a little laugh. "You're right. He was driven by

his ego. It isn't always like that, though. In other families it's more about family and belonging. But in Kevin's case, it was all about him." She huffed a small laugh. "Fortunately, I was 'allowed' to choose their middle names, which are a bit more creative."

"We do this too on Bezchi. Most monarchs will have at least one fledging named with a combination of their names." He blinked a couple of times, then looked down at his wine glass as if he'd said too much.

That was weird. "I've heard about the monarchs on Bezchi. They're elected and rule in pairs, right?"

"That is correct." Kyzel shifted slightly on his bench. "All monarchs from all the clans mate for life. Some clans have a mixture of members who are life mates, and seasonal mates. The Firewing clan does not mate until they find their soulmate." His gaze met hers, sharp with emphasis. "But *all* raptors mate for life."

Every bit of moisture evaporated from her mouth, and somehow magically reappeared in her panties. Goodness gracious, that was such a turn on. If he didn't stop looking at her like he wanted to devour her, she just might haul him onto the table and have *him* for dinner.

"What about you, Robyn?" he murmured. "Would you mate for life?"

Warmth rose to her cheeks, and she couldn't look away from his intense gaze. "For the right guy…."

Somehow, she'd croaked the words out. There was no denying Kyzel was checking all the *right guy* boxes. He even smelled good. Delicious, actually. She inhaled the subtle scent of nutmeg, which she'd always liked, but now was her favorite.

Kyzel covered her hand on the table with his and raised it, stopping next to his mouth. "I would like to be your right guy, Ms. Martin, if you would allow."

Ms. Martin? Allow? He was asking her permission? What a novel concept.

She wet her lips with her tongue. "I think I'd like that, Kyzel."

As long as she didn't go and screw things up.

He smiled and brushed his lips over her knuckles.

Oh, yeah. She was going to do more than try to make this work.

Kyzel stepped through the restaurant's huge double doors and into the warm evening air. It was nice that contorting himself to enter and exit the facility had not been necessary.

He reached for Robyn's hand. The simple act of twining his fingers with hers filled him with a deep sense of rightness. Their conversation at dinner had been deeply personal, not superficial. His children, her children, his hopes and dreams for his people, and her hopes and dreams for the women she worked to help.

But, most of all, she wanted to pursue a relationship.

This was so different to what he experienced with Careene. Yes, he had known some personal details about his mate, but their discussions had been centered on how they could best work together for the good of their people, and their fledglings. He could please her in bed, and she him, but what had he known about what stirred her to great passion?

Nothing.

They had never had a choice about being together. It just was. Both of them had the necessary traits to rule, therefore their mating was inevitable. He had cared for her, yes, but he had never been *in* love with her. How could anyone be in love with someone they did not know? It was sad, but there hadn't even been the potential of that type of love with Careene.

With Robyn, however—

"You must be having some deep thoughts." Robyn's mellow voice drew him back to the present.

"I am beginning to realize how little I know."

"An epiphany moment, huh?" Her chuckle floated on the warm night air. "And here I was afraid the steak tartar wasn't settling well with you."

He gave her the biggest grin possible. "First, your aunt's cinnamon rolls, then the Polish sausage, now the most perfectly done steak. If I keep eating so well, I will not be able to get off the ground."

A flash of headlights from a car pulling up in the driveway shimmered over the wall of the restaurant for a brief moment.

"Well, we don't want that to happen. I actually like flying with y—" She stopped walking. "Oh, no."

"What is it?" He followed her gaze to the male exiting the newly arrived bright red car, which seemed to be missing its roof.

The male was a stranger to Kyzel, but the way Robyn puckered her lips and squished her nose like she had tasted something sour showed she not only knew him, she also did not hold him in high esteem.

"That's Kevin," she muttered.

"The mate you parted with?"

"One and the same."

"Do you wish me to intercede?" He had no true claim to do so—not yet anyway.

"No. I got this." She faced the approaching male as though prepared for battle.

Kevin did not appear to be hostile—he was even smiling—but why take the chance? Kyzel fanned his right wing out far enough to cover Robyn's back. It was a subtle yet effective way to let the male know he would defend her.

"Hey, Robyn." Kevin waved a hand in a friendly manner as he approached. Interesting how some things were universal. "How are you?"

"I'm fine, Kevin. What's going on?" There was a barely detectable undercurrent of wariness in her words.

The man's grin faltered a fraction, then returned with full force. "Heading in to make a dinner reservation. I, um," he clasped one hand behind his neck and his smile took on a sheepish quality. "I took your advice."

Robyn seemed bewildered. "What advice?"

"I went out last night and, well…" He shrugged his shoulders. "I met someone."

"You *did*?" This news seemed to bewilder Robyn, or was that disappointment?

"I did." He shook his head and chuckled. The short under-feathers at the base of Kyzel's scalp quivered. "I know, I know. I always thought you were it for me, but…, well, when I struck up a conversation with Raven, something weird happened. We just seemed to have a lot more in common than you and I ever did. Made me start thinking, you know?"

"That's great, Kevin."

Robyn sounded sincere, yet no Bezchian male could have such a quick reversal of such deep-seated feelings. Of course, Kevin was not Bezchian, and Robyn was not questioning it, so perhaps it was possible for humans.

Kevin turned and met Kyzel's gaze as he extended his hand. "Hi. I'm Kevin Donahue, the asshole ex, who promises not to be such an asshole anymore."

Kyzel clasped the other man's hand in the Earth greeting of a handshake. "I am Kyzel Raptorclaw. Pleased to meet you."

Good thing he had paid attention during the culture and etiquette videos the agency had sent. Kevin's grip was firm, but not overly so, as the vids had stipulated. It was possible that the male was being more honest than Kyzel credited him.

They released hands, and Kevin nodded his head in the direction of the restaurant's front doors. "Well, good to see you again, Robbi. I'd better go before all the good seats for tomorrow book up."

"Yeah. See ya, Kevin."

Robyn watched Kevin stroll into Snodgrass's, then quirked up one corner of her mouth. "Well. That was interesting."

"Do you think he is speaking true?" Kyzel's question was laced with doubt, and who could blame him?

"I kinda wondered at first, and would still be skeptical if he'd used a more common name like Susan or Debbie; but, Raven? That's not a name that would ever be on his radar." Not in a million years.

Case and point, the names he'd picked for their kids. Well, that was all water under the bridge. Hopefully Raven wasn't a prostitute or something. But that wasn't her problem now, was it?

"Where is the roof of his car?"

"The roof…oh, that." She waved her hand in the direction of the little two-seater. "It's called a convertible; the roof retracts so you can drive around and feel the wind in your hair. Kevin bought this one a year ago."

And immediately drove to her place to *take her for a ride*. Like she'd ever fall for that one.

The warmth of a large, gentle hand against the small of her back drew her attention to Kyzel. The lingering remains of the sunset gave his headfeathers and wings a faint coral glow, but it was the intensity and focus of ice blue eyes that sent a flutter through her.

"I think flying is more fun."

"So do I." She ran her tongue over her lips, and his gaze riveted on it.

It was time to make a choice; end the evening here, catch a cab and go home alone, or have him take her home and see what happened. It'd been so long since she'd invited a man over, but Kyzel wasn't just a man. There was something comfortable about him, about being with him.

For the first time since she'd walked away from her miserable marriage, she didn't want to be alone. Not tonight.

Not again.

She ran her finger over the silky shirt he'd called an omlek and pressed forward. "Let's go back to my place for a nightcap."

Kyzel's feathered widow's peak furrowed. "What is a nightcap?"

"Drinks, talk." She gave her shoulders a shrug and peered up at him through her glasses. "Something more."

Oh gosh, she was coming onto him, and it felt...good. Great, even. A shiver of anticipation coursed through her, settling snuggly in her privates. And just a little bit naughty.

His expression heated and he nodded. "I would like that very much."

Yes, so would she.

TWELVE

---✦---

Kyzel maneuvered his wings, threading himself through Robyn's front door as her hands seemed to touch him everywhere all at once. Tugging at him like she believed he could not get inside her home fast enough. And he could not.

The flight from the restaurant had been the fastest, yet the longest of his life. Holding her against his chest, the feel of the soft, crinkly fabric of her outfit under his fingers, the silkiness of the loose strands of her hair against his face, the always-present vanilla scent that was all hers, had filled him with unparalleled desire. And then she had started nibbling his flesh just below his ear with her blunt teeth….

It had been unbelievably challenging to focus on flying with his cock fully erect. Yet somehow, he had managed to get them to her nest without crashing.

He stumbled into her living room to her shout of triumph, followed by the bang of the front door closing behind him.

"The bedroom's that way." She pointed somewhere behind him with one hand, and flipped the electrical switch next to the door into the down position with the other. "You go, I'll be right there."

"Where are you going?"

"To turn on the kitchen light. I'll be there before you're halfway through the door. Go."

Why the kitchen light mattered was a mystery, but who was he to argue when she told him to meet her in *her* bedroom? He moved toward the partially open doorway, and she was back at his side as he drew his second wing through.

"Omlek," She plucked at his shirt. "How does it come off?"

"Side fasteners…and over the head."

Together they fumbled with the fasteners, punctuated with clumsy hand-bumping and more than a few chuckles, until the final one came free.

"Sit on the bed and pull in your wings."

He moved backward a step at a time, until his legs came in contact with the soft bedcovering. The ends of his wing feathers dragged over the blue and white fabric as he lowered himself to sit on the edge.

Robyn tugged, and he pushed, at the omlek, and it was off in seconds. The cooler air of the room caressed his overheated skin.

The light touch of her small hands over his nipples raised bumps across his flesh. "I've wanted to taste these from the moment you showed up on my front porch."

She ran the flat of her tongue—hot and wet—over each in turn, then nipped at them, sending a stab of passion straight to his groin.

"Robyn." Her name was a rough growl in his throat.

"Too many clothes," she murmured against his chest as her hands gripped the band of his leggings.

He could not agree more, and closed his hands over hers, pushing down to free his erection. Robyn's soft gasp sent a fresh wave of yearning over him.

Focus. On her.

She stared at his appendage with an open mouth and teary eyes. "Lord almighty."

Uncertainty gripped him. "Is something…not right?"

Ah, the feel of her fingertips tracing lightly up his length stole his breath.

She raised her gaze to meet his, and there was nothing but heat in her blue eyes. "Everything is just perfect."

As it turned out, good things *did* come to those who wait. And she'd waited her whole life for a guy who was the total package. In every way, it seemed. Kyzel was sweet, compassionate, attentive, sexy, and he had…. Well. There were some things she would not be telling Meryl about.

"You're in such amazing shape." She walked her fingers over the smooth skin of his defined abs like they were the yellow pages.

"It makes it easier to fly." Kyzel cupped his large hand around the nape of her neck. "Come here."

She leaned in to kiss him as she wrapped her fingers around the velvet hardness of Kyzel's… she wasn't quite ready to call it a dick yet, although she might eventually. It was longer than her hand, thicker at the base, and came to a wide, blunt point. No foreskin or circumcised head, but evenly spaced ridged rings pulsed seemingly in response to her touch.

He groaned against her mouth, and she clenched. Menopausal dryness was not going to be a problem with Kyzel plowing her field.

Goodness, where had that wicked thought come from? Did she care? Not really. She'd never done wicked before, and right now she loved the sound of it.

She broke the kiss and bent close to his tip. "Wicked."

Ooh, the word sounded even better whispered. She swirled her tongue over the bead of precum.

Kyzel growled above her. Then her feet left the floor and she was back up against the bedroom door, her legs wrapped around his hips, and his tongue thrusting into her mouth. She met his burst of aggression with her own, rocking her hips up and down as the heat of his hardness threatened to scorch away the fabric of her pantsuit.

Way too many clothes.

"Kyzel…."

He seemed to understand what she was getting at, because his went to her waist and worked the knot of the sash loose. A few moments and a flurry of their hands freed her from her outfit and underwear, and him from his pants. Then she stood, bare to him, except for her very sensible one-inch black sandals.

If only she'd kept up her gym membership.

His scalding gaze traveled down her less-than-perfect body and back up. "You are breathtaking."

And he looked…like a predator hunting his prey with his wings half extended. "Really?"

"Really. Don't ever doubt it, my song."

She caught her bottom lip between her teeth. "Can you lay on your back?"

"Yes, but not this time." He closed his hands around her biceps and lifted her up until she could look down at him. "This time I want you wrapped around me and against the door."

There *was* a God, and He'd heard all her prayers. And, was that her breathing so raggedly? Must be, because Kyzel was busy tracing his tongue along a silvery stretch mark on one breast now. His hot mouth closed over the pink, puckered nipple and drew it in rough enough to send an arc of electric lust into her core. A cry of utter pleasure came from somewhere deep inside her.

She gripped his shoulders and arched her back, offering herself to him. "I want you so hard."

His growl vibrated through her and he lowered her until his tip bumped against her entrance. She wrapped her legs around him, and the light tickle of his wing feathers brushing her thighs added fuel to the fire. Then he was pushing into her, slowly. So much control, so much stretching, so much filling, so much...everything. More than she ever experienced before. All her channel muscles contracted and released around him, as though cheering him on.

He murmured something she didn't understand, but the sentence ended with her name so it must be good.

"Don't stop." She ran her tongue along the smooth underside of the shell of his ear.

He slid his hands downward, and gripped her butt, then pulled back and slammed into her again, and again, and again, rocking her into the door as a blissful pleasure built.

She bucked her hips forward to meet him, each time bringing her closer to a level of oblivion that had always just eluded her. Kyzel increased his tempo, and his grunt next to her ear sent her spinning off a ledge.

"Kyzellll!"

She clamped down around him as stars exploded in her vision.

Kyzel thrust hard, arching into her as he released. A fluttering sensation ran up and down her walls, tickling her g-spot. The rings around his shaft, maybe? Dear God, whatever was happening it was extending her climax on and on and….

She opened her mouth and released the building scream of gratification into the room, then collapsed against his body.

Drained. Spent. And utterly sated.

THIRTEEN

———◆———

Meryl gripped the steering wheel of her car. She really shouldn't do a slow drive-by of Robyn's house, but what if, despite the odds, her date had imploded? Robyn might need a pep talk, or some wine, or….

Just admit it, Meryl, you're dying of curiosity.

And there was nothing wrong with that. What kind of friend would she be if she didn't at least check? It wasn't like she was going to stop by…unless both the porch and kitchen lights were on. That was their secret signal that a date was over, and it was time to talk.

Robyn's house came into view. The porch light was off and the kitchen light on—for the first time in the five years since her bestie had been divorced. Date night was still going, please do not disturb.

Meryl allowed herself a giddy cackle. *Ooh, Robbi, you naughty, naughty girl.*

A large shadow lurking next to the tall hedge caught her attention. "What in the ever-loving hell?"

That conniving busy-body, Rol met her gaze and…he did

not just shake his head at her, did he? Oh, she was so taking the guy down. Right now.

She pulled the car to the curb, got out—closing the car door gently until it clicked so as not to alert Robyn—and marched across the street. For whatever reason, Rol strode toward her, his long-limbed frame relaxed. But his maddeningly impressive wings were high and half open, a giveaway that he was expecting, and prepared for, a confrontation.

She arrived under the pool of LED white lamplight at the same time he did. As if they'd entered a boxing ring, ready to go a few rounds. "What are you doing here?"

"Checking on my friend—much the same as you, I suspect."

Okay, he had her there. "Except you're probably not as happy about the outcome as I am."

"What do you mean?"

"Oh boy, are you going to be disappointed." She shouldn't smirk, but she couldn't help it.

The corners of his full lips went down. "Explain."

"Well…" she made a stabbing motion in the direction of the porch with her finger, "…Robyn and I have secret signals on date nights. See how the porch light is turned off and the kitchen light is on? That means we're pulling an all-nighter."

"An all-nighter?"

"I think you can figure out what that means."

He blinked down at her as though trying to work out what she'd told him, then his brow creased on either side of his widow's peak. And there was the light of comprehension dawning. "Your friend has enticed Kyzel into her bed, then."

"Wow. Isn't that just like a man, to blame the woman?"

"You do not want to see the truth of the matter because she is your friend."

"I wonder how *your* friend would feel if he knew how little you think of his ability to make his own choices."

Rol opened his mouth, then abruptly shut it again.

You've been schooled, buddy. So why wasn't the sense of triumph settling well with her?

Rol folded his arms over his chest—just like a guy—and glared down his nose at her. Another guy thing. "I will do what I must to protect my friend."

"And I'll do the same for Robyn." She stepped closer, and even the distant freeway noise seemed to quiet in anticipation of her next words. "And I wasn't kidding. If you ruin this for her, I'll find a way to make you pay."

He didn't give so much as an inch, dammit. But as long as he stood his ground, so would she. No matter that his warm, masculine scent tickled her nose with a hint of allspice. No matter that the urge to lean into him was battling with her pride. No matter that the insanity of pressing her lips to his suddenly didn't seem quite so insane anymore.

But it *was* insane. All of it. If she didn't walk away, she'd—

Rol shook his wings, and they settled into place. "Good evening, Ms. Faulkner."

He spun away and strode down the sidewalk. The stride turned into a jog, then a run, then he pumped his massive wings and leaped into the air. He was airborne, a shadow above the streetlights disappearing into the night, leaving behind a small tornado of dead leaves.

And her.

"Jesus, Meryl." She pressed her palm to her chest. If she didn't, her heart might pound its way out. "What the hell was that all about?"

A delicious warmth cocooned Robyn as awareness stole over her, pulling her from the deepest, most sound sleep she'd ever had. At least, as an adult. A comfortable weight rested across her waist. With each breath she inhaled the scent of nutmeg, and the softest blanket whispered over her bare skin like downy feathers.

"Mmm." *Feathers.*

She forced her eyes open. Kyzel was there, lying on his stomach watching her with an expression of utter peace, as if he'd found heaven. And she couldn't disagree. It was like heaven waking up to find him still here, with his arm draped over her and his wing covering her body, sheltering her from the outside world until she was ready to face it again.

And she was nowhere near ready for that, not after all the things they'd done together in the dark of night. The taste of his essence on her tongue, the heat of his mouth sucking her clit. All those deliciously sore muscles clenched and her breath hitched. A thousand more times would not be enough.

Kyzel's peaceful smile widened, and he scooted his lean body toward her. "Good morning, my song."

"Good morning." She rolled onto her back as he followed, and she wrapped her legs around his hips.

His hard, full…dick—yes, dick, she could say…or think…that now—slid into her easily this time, and her moan of pleasure mingled with his. She could get used to being constantly turned on for this guy. That whole *mates for life* thing was sounding better than ever.

She ran her palms over his shoulders and along the arch of his wings. "Soft."

A shiver passed through him. Then his mouth was on hers, their tongues mating as he increased his tempo. Heat built at the source of their intimate friction, and, dear God, everything inside her tightened as each stroke brought her closer to breaking.

She closed her fingers around the edges of his wings and pushed her hips up, meeting him thrust for thrust until her inner walls clamped down around him, stealing her breath as her release washed over her.

"Yessss."

He groaned and surged deep, his wings extending fully.

A distant *crack* barely registered as his body stiffened and he poured himself into her.

Yep, heaven. She inhaled and exhaled, panting as the magic of making love to this man from another world spun around her, bringing her back down for a landing as smooth and gentle as last night's flights had been.

Kyzel braced his weight on his arms and pressed his cheek to hers. "Do you feel it too?"

Feel it? Her whole body was alive with it, whatever *it* was. "I don't want it to end."

"It does not have to." He pulled back and looked down at her.

"But you'll have to go back to Bezchi at some point."

"Not for a few more weeks."

"Good." She smiled up at him. "Then how'd you feel about going away together next weekend? I can rent a cabin in the mountains for us."

Not the one she and Kevin had sold as part of the divorce settlement, but one higher up, where there were fewer people.

"I would love that." He brushed her hair back with one hand. "Why not sooner?"

Sooner would be her choice too, if only. "I wish. But I have to work. The good news is that I only work Monday through Thursday, so we can leave Friday morning. Or Thursday night."

"I understand. I too have commitments to honor back home, and Rol will probably wish to do some sightseeing. I will be ready to go by Thursday night. Also—" He glanced to his right, and a hint of pink glowed on his cheeks. "—can we get a place with a larger bedroom? I seem to have broken your lamp."

She turned her head, and sure enough, the bulky seafoam green glass lamp was hanging off the far edge of the nightstand by its cord, the body cracked open like an egg. "That does look bad, doesn't it?"

"I am sorry." He sounded so contrite. "If there is a way to fix it—"

"No." She grinned up at him. "I never liked that lamp. It belonged to my mother-in-law, and I only took it with me because I didn't want to spend the money on a new one."

"Then, you are not upset?"

"Nope." She placed her hands on either side of his face. "You mean more to me than an ugly old lamp, anyway. But

I will try to find a place with an extra-large master suite so we don't accidently break someone else's stuff."

The look of relief on his face was almost comical. "I will be more careful in the future."

"Great. Because we still have the rest of today and tonight." She raised her head and pressed her lips against his smooth chin in a quick kiss. "Now, have you ever had strawberry waffles before?"

FOURTEEN

Kyzel strode into the suite he shared with Rol. The last two nights—and days—with Robyn still glowed in his heart, a part of every breath he took. Had he ever been happier, more content, about anything in his entire life? Had anyone woven their way into the very fabric of his soul as she had? Granted, the birth of his heirs had brought its own magic and joy, but it was different to what he shared now with her.

And they would be leaving for a long weekend together in just a few days. He would have to tell her then, reveal who he was. It was no longer prudent to keep that from her.

"You have finally chosen to return." Rol's words penetrated his thoughts. "I will schedule passage on the next—"

"Stop, Rol."

Rol sighed and looked up from the Earth book in his hands. "Can you blame me for being concerned?"

"As my friend, no. But this is my decision to make. Mine and Robyn's."

"A decision that will affect our clan, and, to a lesser degree, Bezchi." Rol snapped the book closed and rose.

"It did not seem to be a problem when we left. What do you wish, Rol? That I abdicate to soothe everyone's ruffled feathers?" That was not his first choice, but maybe it would be best for the clan to elect a new ruling pair.

Rol's eyes widened with shock. "No, I—"

"Then why do you continue fighting my choice?" He curled his fingers into fists.

"Because," a new voice interrupted, "your choice goes against the very traditions you are bound to uphold and protect."

Kyzel turned his attention to the unexpected visitor standing in the doorway to the private rooms. The creases of age lined the male's face and bare arms. Everything else was covered in the Firewing clan's traditional flowing garb. His red headfeathers and wings were covered with a silvery sheen. Yet, despite his age, he stood tall.

Rol gestured halfheartedly toward the newcomer. "Kyzel, this is Elder Kai Firewing."

"Greetings, Monarch Raptorclaw." Firewing inclined his head.

Kyzel crisscrossed his arms, pressing the pulse points of his wrists over his heart, and gave the elder a bow of respect. "Greetings, Elder Kai. To what do I owe the pleasure of your attention?"

Not that he could not guess.

"Curiosity," the elder stated.

Doubtful that was the only reason, but he would play along.

"About Earth?" He reached into his omlek pocket and pulled out the folded piece of paper Robyn had given him.

"I have a list of sights to see from Robyn, a local resident who I am considering as a mate."

Kai narrowed his gaze. "You have caused great consternation amongst the elders, Kyzel of the raptor clan."

How had the Firewing elders found out about his search so quickly? Kyzel cast an accusing glare at Rol, but his friend shook his head. So, Kai's visit was not Rol's doing.

The elder continued. "We are not convinced that your actions are in the best interest of Bezchi. I am here to meet the Earth elder who is assisting you with your…match."

"You mean, Ms. Vogel?" It would be interesting to see how the Silverstar agent would respond to that request. And how would she feel about being referred to as *elder*.

Kai blinked as though mildly confused, or surprised. "Is that the elder's name?"

"Yes."

"Then, you will take me to them."

"As you wish, honorable one." After a quick crash course on the cultural aspects of interacting with Earthlings.

Rol reached over and plucked Robyn's list from his hand. "While you do that, I will go see the sights. After all, I have been entertaining the honorable one for two days while you were otherwise *occupied*."

So, this was why Rol seemed more conflicted now. The elder must have fed into his doubts all weekend. Curse it all. He would need to stay alert around the old phoenix.

"Sounds fair, but our discussion is not over."

Rol dipped his head. "As you wish, my monarch."

It was a shame to lose valuable time to change Rol's perspective, but finding a distraction for the elder before the male tried to match him with someone else was a more pressing issue.

"I swear to God, Robyn, you've been smiling all morning."

Robyn met her supervisor's gaze. "No, I haven't."

Jayla's grin stretched across her broad face like she'd figured out the meaning of life, the universe, and everything. "Must've been quite a weekend."

Well, I guess Kyzel was right about my face being expressive.

Or Jayla was just too astute. But dang if all that happiness would stay bottled up. "It was nice."

She opened her wallet and pulled out a twenty.

"Pfft. More than nice, I think, but I can wait. I'll get it out of you eventually." Jayla cackled with glee.

You only think *you will.* Robyn put the wallet back in her purse and gave the drawer a push. The metal glides screeched in unison as it closed. "I'm going to grab a bite to eat. Be back in thirty."

"I'll be here, waiting." Jayla's grin was almost evil. "See ya."

It didn't take long to pop into Magoo's and pick up a plate of mushu pork, then head along the sidewalk back toward the office.

"Ms. Donahue?"

Robyn turned to face the man coming behind her. Not human, a Bezchian. And not as tall as Kyzel, but she still had to tip her head to meet his gaze. "Yes?"

What interesting eyes he has. One gray, one blue.

He stopped a few feet away, smiling in a friendly sort of way. "I am Rol, Kyzel's friend."

"Oh…oh, yes." Why was *he* here? "How are you?"

"I am well. Your planet is quite interesting." He held up a folded piece of paper. "Kyzel gave me your list of sights to visit, thank you."

Ah, so that's how he'd found her. She'd written the list on a piece of work stationery.

"You're welcome." She glanced behind him. "Is Kyzel with you?"

"An elder arrived from home two days ago. Kyzel is in discussion with him regarding business issues." He gestured in the direction she had been walking. "I do not mean to delay you from your errand. May I walk with you?"

"Sure, of course."

He fell in beside her, keeping a respectful distance. "I am glad I accompanied Kyzel on his quest to replace Careene."

Her feet seemed to trip over themselves. She stopped and stared at Rol, her heart caught in her throat. "What do you mean *replace*?"

Rol pursed his lips as though confused. "I…perhaps I used the wrong word? The internal translator is usually excellent, but occasionally there are mistakes."

That must be it. Even high-tech devices weren't completely infallible.

"I see now why he is so taken by you," Rol continued. "I must admit, I was skeptical about his venture here to find a new mate. After all, he and Careene had been matched by our traditions, and were very happy together. It is only right that he honor his first mate by choosing another so similar."

A small choking sound escaped her. Kyzel really did want to *replace* his first mate with her?

Rol sighed, as though the concept was romantic. "Careene was everything to him, and now because of you, he has the chance to recapture that relationship. Do you know that he told me today that he would give up all his responsibilities back home for you?" Rol chuckled. "Which is ridiculous, of course. He is a vital member of our society, and…are you well, Ms. Donahue?"

No, she wasn't well. She'd fallen for Kyzel, but apparently he hadn't seen her as anything other than the *replacement wife.*

"Ms. Donahue?"

"I…I'm fine." Or, she would be if she could get away from this guy. She took in her surroundings, and her gaze fell on the familiar black lettering on Safe Harbor's door a few steps away. "It was nice meeting you, Rol. I need to get back to work now."

"Yes, of course." He stepped away. "It was a pleasure to meet you, Ms. Donahue."

"Yeah." She ducked into the office without a backward glance.

What a miserable afternoon. Robyn sat in the driver's seat of her car, staring at the cinderblock back wall of the building where she worked. Even over four hours after her run-in with Rol, her head still spun. Probably because she'd spent the entire afternoon trying to pretend everything was fine. That yet another relationship wasn't over before it'd begun.

She really, really needed to talk to someone.

She punched the speed dial on her cell phone and pressed it to her ear.

One ringy-dingy, two ringy-dingies, three—

"So, you finally decided to come up for air." Meryl's voice was like a balm on an open wound.

The floodgates opened and a sequence of sobs bubbled out of Robyn.

"Robbi? Robbi, what's wrong?"

"E-e-everyth-th-thing."

"What? What happened?"

"Kyzel is only in-interested in me bec-c-cause he wants to replace his f-first wife…mate." *Whatever.*

"Who told you that?" Bless Meryl for sounding so mercenary, like she was going to kill whoever hurt her.

"H-his friend, R-Rol." She sniffled.

"That dumb shit."

"You…you know h-him?"

"I've met him, and honey, don't you believe a word he says. He's just jealous."

She wiped the backs of her hands over her eyes. "What do you mean?"

"Just trust me. When are you seeing Kyzel again?"

"Thursday night." She sniffled again. "We were planning to go away for the weekend."

Meryl murmured something, then, "I'm at Kit-Kat's. I'm putting you on speaker phone because she's being a brat."

"Hey!" Kathy protested.

"Okay," Meryl continued, her voice taking on the speaker phone echo.

"Hi, Mom." Kathy's voice filled Robyn's heart with love. She swiped the backs of her hands over her cheeks. "H-hi, honey."

"So," Meryl said. "Here's what you're going to do, Robbi. You're going to go away with Kyzel on Thursday night, as planned. You can talk things out with him then. And if you see Rol in the meantime, punch him in the fucking nose."

"Auntie *Meryl*," Kathy chided. "Hey, Mom?"

Funny how fast these two women could make her feel better. "Yes, honey?"

"Aunt Meryl seems to think this guy is wonderful, but does he make *you* happy?"

"Yes. Yes, he does."

"Good. Then I can't wait to meet him. But after you get back next week will be fine. Okay?"

Aw, she'd done something right raising this little girl into a woman. "Okay. Thank you, my love. See you later, 'kay?"

"'Kay."

She disconnected from the call and dropped her phone back in her purse. Yes, she was going to go on this romantic weekend with Kyzel, and she would darn well talk to him about his "friend." But right now, she had things to do, like pick up something for dinner tonight then go home and scan the rental sites for a place.

She turned the key in the ignition and the engine chugged to life. Everything would be okay.

I hope.

Meryl pressed the disconnect button, then caught her bottom lip between her teeth. She had warned that busy-body winged off-worlder to stay out of Robyn's business, but noooo. He just couldn't do it, apparently.

Now she was forced to run interference, and he only had himself to blame. So, what could she do? It had to be something unexpected, without causing any real harm.

"I see you thinking, Auntie."

Meryl met her goddaughter's shrewd gaze. "So?"

Kit-Kat's laughter filled the tiny apartment kitchen. "That's your *I'm plotting revenge* face."

"No, it isn't." Yes, it was. "You don't suppose Bezchians have bank accounts, do you?"

"Let's try something more…legal."

"Party pooper."

"Prison isn't a party."

She gave a snort and leaned back in her chair. "It could be, if we shared a cell."

"Well, yeah, there is that." Kit-Kat grinned. "But let's try to stay on this side of the bars. What else can we do? Report him to Silverstar?"

The agency wouldn't, couldn't, do anything. Rol wasn't a client of theirs—wait a goddamn minute. A slow grin tugged the corners of her mouth. "Kit-Kat, I think I have an idea…."

And Kathy had the technical expertise to pull it off.

FIFTEEN

Robyn navigated a grocery cart through the cereal aisle, the front wheel clacking sideways every other step. Thank God for her little support group, Meryl and Kathy. If not for them, she'd have gone home, canceled the weekend with Kyzel, and cried into a bottle of chardonnay, alone.

Good thing Meryl wasn't like Rol, that was for sure. Imagine being jealous enough to try to undermine a friend's love life. What kind of friend did that?

A pretty pathetic one.

That was going to be a hard conversation to have with Kyzel, but if he was serious about a long-term relationship, he needed to know what his friend had done. And that she wasn't going to be the replacement wife. She caught her lower lip between her teeth. What if he didn't want to hear it, though? What if he got pissed off and ended their relationship anyway? A spike of hurt shot through her heart, just like when Rol had cornered her. Hopefully it'd take a lot more than that to—

"Robyn?"

She jerked her head around. "Kevin?"

Her ex grinned as he pushed his own cart closer. "Sorry. Didn't mean to startle you. I thought you didn't grocery shop on Mondays anymore."

She didn't, not since four months after the divorce, because he used to miraculously always be there at the same time. Was he back to his old tricks? "Just came in for a few things."

"Me too." He waved his hand over his cart. "Planning a dinner for two with Raven."

"Oh?" She eyed his items. Potatoes, baked beans, a head of cabbage, two steaks, and a bouquet of pink carnations. Could it be that he really wasn't stalking her this time? "She's a t-bone steak kind of gal, huh?"

Kevin directed a small frown at the steaks. "Actually, I don't know. Why?"

"Depends on how much you want to impress her."

"A lot." He raised his gaze to meet hers. "Should I get something else?"

Not once in five years did she expect to give Kevin advice on how to impress another woman. My, how things changed. "If you're really serious about her, go with a Filet Mignon."

"Really?"

"Yep."

He grinned, and for a moment she glimpsed the guy he'd been when they'd first met. "Thanks, Robbi. I owe you."

"No worries." She gave her hand a wave. "I'm really happy for you."

"Thanks. I'm happy for you too. Who knew you'd bag yourself a royal?"

She blinked at him, her own smile dropping away. "Excuse me, what?"

"Uh, yeah. Your winged off-worlder."

"What about him?"

Vertical worry lines appeared between Kevin's brows. "Don't you know?"

A spark of irritation flared. "Know *what*, Kevin?"

His eyes went wide. "You *don't* know. Oh, shit, Robbi...."

"Tell. Me." She forced the words out between her clenched teeth.

"He's...well, he's one of the four kings of Bezchi, or something like that."

A *king*? He couldn't be. He would've told her, wouldn't he? Kevin must be making it up. "How do you know this?"

"Raven. She works for *Blast off!*. She told me."

"Your new *girlfriend* works for that gossip rag?" The tell-all media outlet for the who's who of off-worlders? Oh, didn't that just figure? "Are you sure she's got a thing for you, or is she looking for a story?"

Kevin gaped, as if that had never occurred to him. A wave of guilt crashed over her. Who was she to destroy another's happiness? Unless he was up to his usual games. No, this was too deep for him.

"I'm sorry, Kevin. I didn't mean it, I'm just a little...shocked. I'm sure Raven's a great person who really cares for you."

"No." Kevin shook his head. "No, you may be right. I thought I was lucky that some babe who's decades younger even noticed me."

Decades? "Kevin...."

"Leave it, Robyn."

She snapped her mouth shut hard enough for her teeth to clack together. He was right, though. There was nothing she could say that'd help.

Kevin made a scoffing noise. "Aren't we just a pair? Both discovering...dammit. I gotta go, maybe drown my sorrows in a bottle of Jack. See ya."

He turned and trudged back up the aisle toward the front of the store and rounded the corner, shoulders slumped like he'd just lost his dog...except he'd never had a dog in his life. Poor guy was hurting bad though, he'd left his shopping basket and food.

Well, she'd walk out too if she wasn't out of milk and sandwich meat at home.

May as well finish my shopping.

She cast a glance at Kevin's abandoned basket. In good conscience, she couldn't walk away and let the food spoil. It would be no big deal to put his items back as she finished her personal shopping. She transferred the steaks, then reached for the baked beans. Beans, *and* cabbage? Really, who gave their new girlfriend beans and cabbage for dinner? Talk about a major dating faux pas.

Wait a minute. She stopped. No one did something like that, unless they were an idiot...which Kevin was, but still.

If he's the idiot, why am I picking up after him again?

That manipulative little twit. Was there even a *Raven* at *Blast off!*? And if he'd lied about that, then was Kyzel really a king? She reached into her purse and fished around until her fingers bumped against her phone. Ah ha. She lifted it out. Time to fact-check at least one of Kevin's stories.

She finger-typed *Kyzel* and *Bezchi* and tapped the search icon. A series of articles and pictures popped up, many of them of Kyzel and a tall, willowy, winged woman.

"Careene." She whispered the name.

Kevin hadn't lied. Kyzel was a monarch, and Careene was stunning with her million-dollar smile and crystal blue eyes. Not a headfeather out of place.

I can't even compete with that.

Her gaze was snagged by a headline, "Monarch Careene passes to the Great Aerie." The accompanying photo was of Kyzel, alone, head bowed, black fabric draped over his magnificent wings. Her heart ached for him.

"Oh, Kyzel."

But he lied to me by omission.

A little hot coal of anger started burning in her chest. Why the heck had he kept that vital bit of information from her? His royal status wasn't a problem, but not telling her about it definitely was. If he had just been up front with her, she would've been more than willing to figure out how to make things work out between them.

Men were all manipulators, no matter what planet they came from. And she was the idiot who fell for it every single time.

I'm so done with this.

Done with being manipulated by Kevin. Done with being manipulated by *King* Kyzel and his little friend. Just done. She transferred the steaks back to Kevin's abandoned cart for someone else to deal with. Someone not named Robyn Martin.

By the time she'd finished her shopping, checked out, and pushed her glitch-wheeled cart to her car, the first doubt had creeped in. What if Kyzel had a reason for not telling her? Why assume the worst without giving him a chance to explain? Her ex didn't have a stellar record in the empathy department, but it wasn't fair to lump Kyzel in with him.

She pushed the key into the trunk lock of her sedan then gave it a twist until it popped open. How had Kevin found out anyway? Maybe *Raven* was real—

An arm snaked around her shoulders, and she was pulled back against a solid male chest. She sucked in a sharp breath of surprise just as a noxious cloth was slapped over her mouth and nose.

"This is for your own good, Robbi."

Kevin. Why?

She let her body go limp to throw him off kilter with her deadweight, but blackness was closing in, and it dragged her into a void of nothingness.

SIXTEEN

Where was Robyn? Kyzel paced the length of the suite's common room. She had not answered her phone last night when he had called. And all his calls today had gone into her voicemail. It was possible she was busy at work and had turned off her phone, but the faint itch between his wings had never let him down before. Something was not as it should be.

"Would you please cease your incessant pacing?" Rol growled.

"I cannot." He shifted and turned on the ball of his foot to move toward his friend.

Rol heaved a sigh and tossed the book he had been reading on the side table. "Why not?"

"My mate seems to be missing."

Rol opened his mouth, then snapped it shut. "Perhaps she is avoiding you."

"Does that sound like normal behavior from someone who invited me to go away with her for a few days this weekend?"

"No. It does not." Rol glanced around the room. "Your friend—"

"Mate."

"—is not the only one missing. Where is Elder Kai?"

"No idea." Kyzel gave a dismissive one-handed wave. "He seemed determined to go out, so I sent Fyad with him."

"He could ignite at any time. Should he not be with us when that happens?"

"As he is an elder, I am certain he can handle his personal situation without our assistance." It would not be the first time a Firewing would do so.

Kyzel paused by the window and gazed out at the pale blue afternoon sky, and the lengthening shadows. It had been several hours since he'd last called. Time to try again. He dug his hand into his pants pocket and closed his fingers around his phone.

"Are you truly calling her again?"

"She is my mate, Rol." He locked his gaze with his friend's and suspicion reared. Did Rol know something? "Why do you ask?"

Rol averted his gaze to the book on the table and shrugged. "What if she is not your mate?"

"She is my mate as surely as you are my friend. You are my friend, yes?"

There was probably nothing in the universe that could refocus Rol's attention on him faster. "Always. Even when we do not see eye to eye."

The sudden feeling of unease faded with those words. "Thank you."

He pulled his phone from his pocket, and his gaze snagged on the screen updates.

New voicemail from Nixy Vogel.

"Ms. Vogel called." He pressed the button to retrieve messages and raised the phone to his ear.

"*Hi, Mr. Raptorclaw, this is Nixy Vogel at Silverstar. Please call me back on my personal line as soon as you can.*"

Hope flared in his chest. Maybe she knew what was going on with Robyn.

He pressed the speed dial for the agency.

"Nixy Vogel." The agent's greeting was threaded with...exasperation?

"Good afternoon, Ms. Vogel. This is Kyzel."

"Kyzel, great. Thank you for getting back to me."

Rol stepped up next to him. "Ask her about Elder Kai."

Why in the fair currents would he do that? Kai was the least of his worries, and certainly not the reason for calling Ms. Vogel.

"Is that Rol?" Ms. Vogel asked. "Tell him I have excellent news—"

"Ms. Vogel." Her name came out sharper than he had intended, and yet not sharp enough. "I am not a messenger service for either of you." He cast a narrow-eyed glare at Rol, who took a step back. "I am calling to alert you that Robyn seems to be missing."

"Missing?" She seemed genuinely taken aback. "No, that's not possible. I received a text from her around twelve thirty this morning."

"You did? What did she say?"

"Erm." Ms. Vogel cleared her throat. "Well, please

understand that in cases like this, the Silverstar Agency will honor—"

"The message, please, Ms. Vogel." He forced the words out between his teeth.

"Yes, of course. Sorry. Ms. Donahue has informed me that she wishes to discontinue her relationship with you and has withdrawn her application from further consideration."

No. Pain lanced through him, and he reached out for the window frame to steady the floor-surging-under-his-feet sensation. This could not be happening. Why would Robyn say such a thing? Why did she not tell him herself?

Rol grabbed him by his biceps. "Kyzel?"

"She…has rejected me." His mate did not want him.

An undetermined emotion flickered in Rol's eyes, and was gone. Surprise, perhaps?

He swallowed hard around the stone of grief in his chest. "Ms. Vogel, did she say why?"

"No. Silverstar does not require an explanation from its clients. No means no, Mr. Raptorclaw. I'm sorry." She did sound very apologetic—not that it helped. "When you're ready, shall I resubmit your profile for a new match?"

"No." The word was like gravel in his throat. "She is the one." *The only one.*

"I understand," Ms. Vogel said. "I will remind you that your contract states you are not to attempt to reestablish contact, is this clear?"

"Yes."

"Good. I'll put you in the inactive file for six Earth months in case you change your mind."

He would not change his mind, nor would he give up so

easily. A sense of determination surged up like a wave and washed away the pain.

"All right." But there was nothing right about this situation. Not one single thing. "Thank you. Goodbye."

He flicked his thumb over the disconnect button and strode toward the door.

"Where are you going?" Rol sounded mildly panicked.

"To find my mate." It was time to get to the bottom of this situation. "Let Fyad know. I may need his help. Meet me at Robyn's office directly after."

Kyzel paced in the darkness, the swish of his sandaled feet through the emerald green grass in Robyn's front yard seemed to say, *"Wesh, wesh, wesh."* Gone, gone, gone. But to where? She had not shown up to work today. The lights were off in her nest, and her car was not in her driveway.

"Ms. Donahue has obviously had a change of heart, just as Ms. Vogel stated," Rol reasoned from behind him. "I, for one, believe it is a sign as to the fickle nature of Earthlings."

Robyn was not fickle. He turned and strode back in Rol's direction. A handful of feathers spun and floated around his ankles.

Rol sighed. "You are molting."

Kyzel paused and lowered his gaze to the trail of feathers on the lawn. He raised his wings and snapped them open and closed. Three more feathers fluttered free. Stress molting. It happened sometimes, but never to him.

"Kyzel, listen to reason. You gave it your best wing, but

this experiment did not work. It is time to go home, to find your true mate."

"She *is* my true mate." His shout echoed through the yard. The volume of the incessant night song chirped out by the little Earth insects Robyn called crickets diminished. "I will not leave her. She might be in trouble."

"How could she be in trouble? She texted Ms. Vogel."

"I do not know, Rol. Something is not right about this."

"Yes." Rol stood taller, suddenly full of conviction as the headlights of a passing car flashed over him. "Yes, *something* is not right. Getting involved with Earthlings is not right. Not for you. Not for a monarch."

"How am I any different than you? Or Fyad. Or Elder Kai for that matter?" Except for the lifespan differences between Firewings and the rest of the clans.

"Because you are *our* leader, and you set the example for all Raptorclaws." Rol made a pleading gesture with his hands. "Please, Kyzel. I have stood by you this far. Now it is time to go home."

Kyzel stepped close to Rol, nearly nose to nose. "I. Am. Not. Leaving."

"Hey!"

Kyzel turned toward the unexpected voice.

Meryl slammed her car door and marched toward them. "What the hell is going on here? Why are you guys having it out in the dark in Robyn's front yard?"

Relief coursed through him as Robyn's friend approached. "Do you know where she is?"

The question seemed to startle her. "I thought she'd be with *you*."

"I have not seen her since yesterday morning." Looking beautiful as the morning sunlight had danced over her pale hair. When had he become so poetic? "And her supervisor said she was not at work today."

The woman had stayed late to cover Robyn's caseload.

True concern shone in Meryl's eyes. "That doesn't sound like her. Did Jayla say anything else?"

"She said Robyn was happier than she'd ever seen her yesterday morning, but quiet and withdrawn after lunch. She did not know why, though." Somehow the change in her demeanor had to be linked to her disappearance.

"This is *your* fault." Meryl moved like a predator toward Rol, eyes flashing with anger, teeth bared. "You just couldn't leave her alone, could you?"

Rol's eyes widened and he took a step back, but there was no escaping the demoness Meryl had become.

"I *warned* you to stay out of their business, but noooo. And now, she's disappeared."

She had warned Rol about what? "Explain, Rol."

Rol sighed. "I intercepted Ms. Donahue yesterday when she was walking back to her office with her lunch."

Meryl made an impatient rolling gesture with her hand. "Go on. Tell him what you told her."

"I mentioned you were looking for a replacement mate." His friend's face darkened as he lowered his gaze to the ground.

"You…you…." The words wheezed out of him. "Why would you *do* that?"

"I…my intent was not to get her to run away, merely discourage her."

Meryl raised her fists as though ready to pummel them against Rol's chest. "But that's exactly what happened. And now no one knows where she is, not even *me*."

Rol grasped her wrists. "I take full responsibility for this, Ms. Faulkner." He met Kyzel's gaze. "I have made a grave error in judgement, kee mohap."

Kyzel curled his upper lip. "Yes, you have."

"Y'wanna help, buzzard breath?" Meryl growled at Rol. "Then *find her*."

Rol shook his head. "I do not know where to begin."

A muffled shriek and the telltale *fwump* of wings beating the air pulled Kyzel's attention to the hedge. Three heartbeats passed before a large shadow rose over the hedge and glided their way.

"What the hell…?" Meryl stepped back, bumping into Rol, who grasped her by her shoulders to steady her.

A moment later, Fyad touched down feet first in front of him, a young Earth female wiggling in his embrace. Her green eyes flashed with anger above the large hand clamped over her mouth. "Greetings, my mon…*sir*."

"Fyad." Kyzel lowered his gaze to the detained female. "Who is this?"

"This is my Earth friend, Raven Crawford. She likes spending time in shrubbery, taking photographs of you with her camera."

"Mmm mmm-mmm." Raven's words might be incomprehensible from under Fyad's hand, but the anger in her tone was not.

Kyzel gave his hand a wave. "Please release Ms. Crawford, Fyad, but do not allow her to escape."

Fyad obliged, moving his hands to the woman's shoulders. She immediately turned on him. "I am sick and tired of you bullying me, you dumbass. I've got a job to do, and you just made me drop my camera."

Meryl jerked like she had suddenly come awake, and yanked herself away from Rol. "What kind of job requires you to skulk around in bushes taking pictures?"

"I work for *Blast off!*, the who's-who in the off-worlder community," Ms. Crawford snapped back.

If knowledge was a sun, then Meryl's expression was a sudden sunrise. She locked gazes with him. "Who *are* you?"

He glanced at Rol, who shrugged, then back to Meryl. "There are four clans on Bezchi. I am the Raptorclaw clan's monarch."

"Well, shii-iit." Meryl frowned. "And you didn't tell Robyn?"

"No."

"Men are idiots."

He was beginning to think so as well. He turned his attention back to Raven.

Meryl waved one manicured hand. "We can deal with that part later. Right now, we need to figure out what happened to Robyn. I'll call her."

Kyzel gave his head a shake. "I have tried that all afternoon. She did not answer." He bent to peer at Raven. "I know you. We saw you on the street the first night we were here."

Raven grinned. "I know. I recognized you from pictures I'd seen."

"And," Fyad rumbled, "you have been following him ever since."

Raven curled her lip, but did not reply.

Kyzel folded his arms across his chest. "Kevin Donahue claims you are his *girlfriend*. Is that true?"

"He *what*?" She seemed genuinely appalled by this information. "No. Gross. Have you seen how *old* he is?"

"Then why would he make such a statement?"

"I don't know. I've only met him once, and that was in the rose garden outside Snodgrass's. I was taking pictures of you at dinner, and he told me your date was his ex-wife. Then he asked about you, and I told him."

Fyad nodded. "I can confirm that, my monarch. She has only had one contact with Kevin Donahue."

"Oh. My. God." Raven twisted partway around in the guard's grip. "You're some sort of sicko stalker, aren't you?"

Meryl turned toward her car. "I'm calling her anyway. She'll answer for me."

Hope soared in his heart. It was possible.

"No, she won't," Ms. Crawford said. "She left town in her ex's car last night."

That could not be. The chirp of the crickets seemed louder in the stunned silence. "Why would Robyn go anywhere with Kevin Donahue?"

"She wouldn't." Meryl glared at Ms. Crawford. "You didn't happen to see which direction they went, did you?"

"East, mostly." Raven shifted from foot to foot. "I'm not sure if she went willingly, though. When Donahue drove past me in the grocery store parking lot, it looked like she was asleep."

"Are you *kidding* me?" Meryl looked like she would

happily strangle the young female. "Did you report it to the police?"

"No."

"Why not?"

"When the girlfriend of an off-worlder monarch leaves town in her ex's car, that screams hot lead. So, I followed them for about three hours until they turned off near the town of Miner's Axe."

"Well, that's just great," Meryl huffed.

"Hey, if it's that late at night and they're still going, it qualifies as a scandal. And that's all I need to do my job."

Kyzel gave her a narrow-eyed glare. "Your job is one of dishonor."

She flinched, but he did not have any more time to waste with her. He turned his attention to Meryl. "What do you know about Miner's Axe?"

"It's a little town about ten miles away from a cabin Robyn and the dickhead owned. They sold it, but he could've rented a cabin nearby."

"Do you have a map?"

"I can print one out at home for you."

"Then we will go to your house and prepare. Fyad, Rol—" He shifted his gaze between the two, "—be ready to fly at first light."

SEVENTEEN

Robyn curled her legs partially under her, huddling into the corner of the old green leather mission-style couch. She'd been here long enough for the hard, wooden armrest to make her elbow ache as she propped her head in her hand.

What a day. She'd slept away most of it, thanks to the chloroform-soaked rag Kevin had used. Then it'd been a battle against dizziness and puking her guts out.

"Please don't be mad, Robbi." Kevin's voice stabbed through her brain. "I couldn't stand by and let you make such a big mistake."

There were so many ways to respond to that statement, and all of them clawed for release. "By kidnapping me?"

"It's a *rescue*."

She gave her hand a little brush-off wave.

"Did I tie you up or throw you in the trunk? No."

"Because knocking me out and bringing me here against my will is so different." Back to the cabin they'd sold as part of the divorce settlement. Never in a million years would she have suspected him of buying it back from the new owners, but he'd claimed he had. "And you took my phone."

"For your own good."

You just keep telling yourself that. "Where is it, anyway?"

"In a gas station garbage can."

"You're crazy." That phone had been her ticket to texting Kyzel for a lift once she escaped.

"I'm *not* crazy."

And an addict can quit anytime.

"Don't worry, Robbi. I texted that woman at the alien hook-up place before I dumped your phone. That winged freak won't bother you again."

A scream stuck in her irritated throat and she buried her face in her hands. There went every hope of an airlift out of the wilderness. She'd have to depend on her own wits to survive until she found a phone to call Kyzel with. When was the last time she'd see a public pay phone anyway?

"Sorry about the chloroform. Do you want to try some toast now?"

No, she wanted to go home, right now, and the only way that would happen was if she lulled him into a sense of complacency. "Fine."

The rustle of Kevin getting out of the chair across the coffee table from her was as annoying as a kid crinkling an empty plastic water bottle.

His footfalls stopped next to her. "Believe it or not, I only want you to be happy."

But I was *happy. With Kyzel.*

She swallowed hard to keep the words from spilling out. It didn't matter, because she had no idea how to be a queen.

Besides, she had obligations here on Earth. Her kids, the women who depended on her at Safe Harbor....

Would Kyzel think she'd ditched him and take the next spaceship home? Or would he have the agency hook him up with someone else? Just the thought of that twisted her heart.

Somehow, he just *had* to figure out she'd been Shanghai-ed. Or Meryl. Jayla would have for sure noticed that she hadn't shown up for work today.

The sounds from the kitchen meant Kevin wasn't in the room with her anymore. If only she felt better, she'd attempt a run for the door.

Be patient.

She peered out between her fingers. The old cabin hadn't changed a bit. All the furniture they had bought years ago still filled the living room with homey comfort.

The small oak dining room table and chairs were a throwback to the early years of their marriage—their first dining set, a gift from Kevin's parents, moved to the cabin when Kevin decided to replace it with a hideous, ultra-modern black lacquer set. It was so ugly; she'd been more than happy to let him keep it after the divorce.

Guess the new owners hadn't been inclined to replace anything. Just as well, because the eclectic casualness was perfect for a mountain setting.

"I lit the fire." Kevin placed a plate of toast on the coffee table.

Did he seriously expect her to be grateful? She raised her head. The dizziness had subsided to a manageable level. She inhaled the buttery scent of the toast and her stomach rumbled. Three pieces seemed a little excessive, but maybe she could eat them all.

Kevin took his seat in the chair again. "Just like old times, eh?"

"Yeah." Just like old times, with him watching and directing her every move. Him controlling her actions, and her waiting for the chance to slip away.

She picked up the first slice of toast between her thumb and forefinger. "How long are we staying?"

"Until you come to your senses."

Oh, I've already done that.

But the more Kevin believed she was malleable, the more likely she could affect her escape plan. Her gaze caught on the glass goblet of ruby red liquid sitting next to her plate. He had brought her a glass of *wine*?

"You've had a trying day," he crooned. "You've earned it."

"I can't even. Not feeling like I do." She bit into the toast, savoring the satisfying crunch as she chewed.

"You're wasting a perfectly good glass of wine, you know. It's your favorite."

"No, Kevin, it's not my favorite. It's *your* favorite. I prefer whites to reds, which I've told you more times than I can count." He still never listened to her. "So, please, feel free to drink *my* wine."

Besides, there was no telling if he'd put anything in it to keep her drugged.

Kevin flopped back in his chair and glowered at the dancing flames. As nice as it was that he'd stopped talking, it meant he was trying to cook up some other way to keep her under control.

She chewed and swallowed the last piece of toast, then brushed her fingers over her plate. "Thank you."

"Do you want some more?"

"No." Three slices had filled her.

"Yes, you do. Relax, babe, I got you." He reached for her plate.

"Seriously, Kevin?" She planted her fists against the smooth warm leather cushion and pushed herself to stand. "I'm going to bed now."

She turned and marched toward the hallway beyond the cozy kitchen where the bedrooms were. The faint creak of leather and the rustle of clothing came from behind her. Darn man was following her. Still so predictable.

At the bathroom door, she spun to face him. "No, you are not following me into the bathroom."

"How do I know you won't climb out the window and run back to that loser?"

"Why would I do that?" Other than to get away from her now certifiably insane ex. "He *lied* to me, remember?"

Kevin pursed his lips together, uncertainty in his mud brown eyes. Eyes that were so different from Kyzel's clear blue ones.

A little more convincing couldn't hurt. She lay her hand on his forearm. "Seriously, could you see me as the queen of anything?"

A little of the uncertainty faded.

"Besides, you know how I feel about the nighttime forest critters."

Kevin visibly relaxed. "Fine. I'll trust you for now, but I won't be far."

Of course he wouldn't be, and that's why she wouldn't be escaping right now. She stepped into the bathroom and closed the door, shutting out Kevin and all the negativity he represented.

"There are toothbrushes in the top drawer," Kevin said through the crack of the door.

Right where she'd always kept them. Guess he wasn't lying about having bought the cabin back. "Thank you."

She was being nicer to him than he deserved. If she could beat him over the head with her fists for being such an idiot, she would.

She took her time with her bedtime ablutions, then braced herself to face him again. She pulled the door open and stepped out of the bathroom.

Kevin was back in the living room, his chair now angled so he could see straight down the hall to the door of the master bedroom. No surprise there. Sadly, her purse was still MIA. Not much could be done about that.

"Good night, Kevin."

"Good night, Robyn."

The old brown shag carpet muffled her footfalls. At the bedroom door she turned and met his gaze. "I guess Raven isn't real."

"Oh yes, she is a real person." One corner of his mouth quirked up in a smirk. "I met her, she does work for Blast off!, and she's the one who told me the winged creep is royalty."

Well, knock her over with a feather. That wasn't what she'd expected to hear. Now it was more important than ever that she didn't react. He might mistake that for interest and try to keep the conversation going.

She gave him a nod, stepped into the room, then closed the door. The click of the latch into the strike plate seemed too loud. Like a prison door locking.

Kyzel circled, floating on the gentle morning air currents. At this altitude, the sun was visible over the mountain range, yet below him, the sleepy gray-greens of the valleys and west-facing peaks still awaited the warm touch of Earth's yellow star.

But the darkness of the crevasses was no impediment to his hunting vision. Nature had blessed him with an adaptive lens within his eyes, a genetic enhancement from a time when his people had hunted to survive. Never in all his sun migrations had he expected to use it to locate an alien mode of transport on another planet. Yet here he was, flying in a search pattern of ever widening circles. To the south and the north, Rol and Fyad did the same.

He passed over the black highway again. The cabin-nest Meryl had spoken of must be close; it was just a matter of time until he found it. Time and focus.

A thin cloud of dust wafted up, drawing his attention to a stand of trees. It was from a gravel driveway in front of a tent-shaped roofline, but the vehicle that had created the dust was gone—probably on the paved road somewhere now.

His gaze followed a thin veil of residual dust along the road leading back to the highway. There, a flash of red…it was the same car Kevin Donahue had driven at the restaurant. The roof was up this time, making it difficult to tell if there were one or two passengers inside—which did not matter. If Robyn was there, he would get her out and take her home. If she was not, then her ex-mate would tell him where she was.

With the road being a winding one, it was no trouble getting ahead of Donahue. Kyzel angled his wings and hurtled downward toward the car. Five…four…three…he pushed out his wings, slowing his descent.

Boom!

The hood cracked with the force of the impact, and a scream from cornered prey shattered the morning's air. Kyzel curled his fingers around the edge of the hood in front of the windshield and extended his talons to keep his grip. He blinked back to normal vision, and met Donahue's wide-eye stare. Donahue…alone…no passenger. The man clung to the steering wheel; his knuckles white. The scent of fear emanated from the Earthling. Fear would lead him to desperation, and eventually a fatal mistake.

Donahue yanked the steering wheel left and right in an attempt to dislodge him. Kyzel curled his lip in a sneer at the desperate male. Then Donahue jerked the directional control wheel of the vehicle hard to his left and the car spun one hundred eighty degrees —*boom!*—into a tree. The passenger door caved in so far it seemed like the car was giving the tree a hug.

Rage filled him. If Robyn had been in the car, the fool would've killed her. He released his grip, slid off the hood, and gave Donahue a death stare through the cracked glass.

"Where is she, Donahue?"

"Look what you did to my car, you fucking prick." Spittle flew from the fool's mouth.

There was no sense in wasting any time here. Kyzel slammed his talons into the roof fabric and sliced it open to expose the rot within the vehicle.

"What the fuck?" Donahue screamed the words, but there was no one on the lonely mountain road to hear. Except Kyzel. "What are you doing, you crazy alien bastard?"

Kyzel leaped onto the ravaged remains of the car and grabbed the man's flailing arms. Then he gave his wings a flap to expedite dragging Donahue back over the trunk and onto the gritty road shoulder. An odd name for the strip of dirt bracketing roads on this planet.

"Again. Where. Is. She. Donahue?"

"Fuck you." Donahue's boot-heel connected with Kyzel's shin and he inhaled sharply at the pain and released his adversary.

The time for mercy was over. He turned away, counting off his steps. At twenty, he faced Donahue again and raised his hands, talons fully extended. "You will tell me everything."

It had not seemed that the Earthling's eyes could open any wider, but Donahue disproved that theory. Kyzel gave him a grim smirk, took a step, then another, moving toward the man faster and faster.

"No. No—oh, fuck." Robyn's ex scrambled for purchase in the dirt, gaining his feet.

But there would be no escape for the raptor's prey today. He sank his talons into the man's shoulders then gave his wings several full beats. The human's flailing and weight was enough to bobble the take off, but experience gave Kyzel the advantage. A moment later, Donahue was safely huddled in the crown of a forty-foot pine tree, blood oozing from the talon wounds. Well, as safely as he could be, given the circumstances.

Kyzel alighted on the branch of the next tree over. "Now, we talk."

"You're a fucking maniac!"

"It is true. Such is our way when our mates are in danger."

"I have nothing to say to you." The man was the epitome of obstinacy.

"Perhaps I should leave you to reconsider your position...no pun intended, of course."

Malevolence shot like darts from Donahue's eyes. "Fuck you, freak."

Well, there was nothing else to do. "All right, then. I will return after mid-day and we can continue this conversation."

He rose and balanced on the branch, then unfurled his wings.

"*Wait.*"

It was all he could do to beat back a grin of triumph. "What?"

"She climbed out the bedroom window and ran away last night."

"You forced her into your bed?" The words slipped out before he thought to stop them.

"I didn't have to force her." Donahue did not hide his malicious grin. "You don't really think she run off with a freak like you, do you...especially after I told her you kept a very important secret from her?"

Regret sank its talons into his heart.

"That's right," Donahue gloated. "I told her about your

royal title. She don't wanna be your queen, that's what she told me last night. She wanted *me*."

"If she truly wanted you, she would not have climbed out the window."

Donahue snapped his mouth shut. No, Robyn had not shared his bed—willingly, or not.

Kyzel regarded his opponent. "Why are you not out looking for her?"

"I *was*." The lie reeked of sourness. "That's where I was going when you wrecked my car."

"Of course, you were." He braced himself for a jump, bunching his legs under him. "I will send someone for you, *if* I find Robyn alive. And you best hope I do, otherwise it will not go well for you."

He pushed off the branch, first diving, then swooping upward, catching the still-crisp mountain currents. Behind him, Donahue's angry shouts faded with distance.

Had a truck-stop ever looked so wonderful? Robyn stumbled forward from under the trees and blinked hard as tears blurred her vision of the giant asphalt parking lot. Trucks, tour buses, cars, and people. Who would've thought she'd ever be so happy to see any of them?

Now, if someone would loan her a phone, she could call Meryl to come pick her up here. Wherever here was.

She gave her cheeks a back-handed swipe. Stupid tears.

"Ma'am?"

She turned, and blinked at the young man halfway out of the cab of a semi.

"Are you okay?" He hopped down.

"Do you have a phone?"

"Yeah, sure."

Oh, thank goodness. That was easier than she'd expected.

The trucker pulled a cell phone from his pocket and handed it to her. "Sorry, but you look like you spent the night in the woods."

"Not the whole night, just since three a.m."

"Do you need me to call an ambulance—?"

"No." The startled look on his face confirmed she'd spoken too harsh. "I'm sorry. I just want to call my friend to come pick me up."

He nodded. "That's cool, that's cool."

"Thanks." She gave him as much of a smile as she could muster, then pressed the numbers and raised the phone to her ear.

EIGHTEEN

---*---

Three days later.

Robyn sat at her dining table, twirlin Kyzel's wing feather between her thumb and forefinger. Even after all these days the scent of nutmeg was still there, as strong and pleasant as it'd been the day she'd found it on her porch. As if he was in the room with her.

But he wasn't. He hadn't been since the day she'd come home. The day she'd told him she couldn't go with him to Bezchi. Couldn't be his mate, or his queen.

And today, he was leaving, going back to Bezchi. Her heart seemed to fold in on itself like a desolate child in the fetal position. Broken. Shattered. If everything had gone like it was supposed to, she and Kyzel would be in the mountains right now. Just the two of them.

She had made the right choice, hadn't she? Bezchi was no place for a wingless human who didn't know squat about it or its people.

Okay, that wasn't entirely true. She had done a lot of research in the past few days, and Kyzel's people and planet sounded like her tribe. But, how could she leave her kids?

Or the women who turned to her and the shelter for help.

"Mom." Kathy slid her hands around hers. "It's not too late. He doesn't leave until noon."

Less than two hours. She exhaled softly. "I know. I've been watching the clock since two a.m."

"C'mon, Mom. After what Dad did, you still want to hang out here?"

"The restraining order will cover that, honey."

"It takes three weeks just to get the hearing. In the meantime, you don't have a twenty-four-hour security guard to make sure he stays away."

"I don't need a guard—"

"Maybe not now, but eventually. You *know* how he is."

"Kathy, please…."

"But there's no reason for you to stay." Her daughter continued on as if she hadn't heard her plea. "I have told you we'll all be fine. Even Auntie Meryl agrees. You can visit us, and we'll come visit you."

"No, that's not it. I love you and your brother and sister, but you are all self-sufficient adults."

Kathy shook her head. "I don't get it. What's keeping you from finding happiness for yourself?"

"My job." She leaned forward in her chair. "Honey, there are people out there, women, who are in worse situations than I ever was. And I'm in the position to be able to help them, to get them into safe places, get them jobs. I can make a—"

Bang, bang, bang.

The booming knock at the front door was as startling as it was a relief. "Hang on a sec. Let me see who's there."

She slid her hand from between Kathy's and pushed out of the chair.

Her daughter slumped back in her chair; her lips pursed in a sour pout. "Probably Dad."

God, don't let it be Kevin. Although, it wouldn't surprise her. Maybe Kathy was right, and the restraining order wouldn't be enough. She could literally be walking into his grip right now.

She peered through the newly installed peek hole. *Is that a man nipple?*

Her heart fluttered to life again and she yanked on the doorknob a little harder than normal. The heat of the late summer morning rolled over her and she tipped her head back. Her gaze met the heterochromatic eyes of the winged man on her porch.

"Ms. Donahue."

"R-Rol?" Not at all the Bezchian she'd hoped to see again.

He nodded. "May I come in?"

"Why?" Well, that was rude of her, but so what.

"There is something very important we must discuss before I leave, and I am not in the position to take no for an answer."

"Oh, really?" The fight wasn't in her, though. She sighed and moved away from the door. "Fine. Come in, then."

It took him a minute to contort his way into the house, but soon enough he was filling the living room in the same dominating way Kyzel had. Only without all the sexiness.

"Ms. Kathy." Rol nodded at her daughter.

Her daughter narrowed her eyes at him. "Hello, Rol."

That seemed to be all the greeting either of them was interested in giving the other.

Rol turned his attention back to Robyn, his wings drooping until the tips brushed the hardwood floor. "My behavior toward you outside your office that day was inexcusable. I have hurt you, and I have hurt my friend and my monarch." He lowered himself to one knee, planted one fist to the floor for balance, then dipped his head. "I have come to apologize and beg your forgiveness."

"Uh." She cast a glance at Kathy and her daughter shrugged. No help there. She redirected her attention to the top of his brown and gray-mottled feather cap. "That was a pretty crappy thing you did."

"Yes." He nodded, but didn't look up. "One I hope to rectify before I leave."

Rectify seemed too optimistic. The act, and the resulting fallout, couldn't be erased, but at the very least she could help him ease the mild animosity between them.

"Okay." She made a shrugging gesture with her hands. "Okay, Rol. I'll forgive you. It may take me a while to look at the incident objectively, but I think you were doing what you thought was right for your people."

And, put like that, it seemed like a small weight had lifted off her shoulders.

Now Rol raised his head and met her gaze. "Thank you, kee mohap. May I rise?"

"Uh, sure." The guy must be feeling pretty sorry to ask her permission to stand up. Or maybe it was a Bezchian thing, being in someone else's nest. Home. Now she was thinking in Bezchian terms.

Rol stood and stared down at her. "My purpose here is twofold."

"Oh? What else is on your mind?"

"Kyzel."

"No—"

"Please, hear me out. My time is limited."

The scrape of the dining chair over the hardwood seemed unusually loud. Kathy stood, leaning forward with her palms flat against the table top. "She'll listen."

"I will?" She fixed her daughter with an incredulous look.

"Mom." There was a finality in her voice, almost identical to the tone Robyn had used with her kids when they were younger.

She raised her hands in a frustrated surrender. "Fine."

Geez, it was like their parent/child roles had abruptly switched.

"Thank you." Rol inclined his head toward Kathy, then his attention was back on Robyn. "I have never seen Kyzel happier than when he was with you. And since the last time he saw you, I have never seen him more devastated. Now, here, I see you and the same sorrow haunts your eyes. You are hurting as much as he. At one time it would have pained me to admit this, but no longer. Kyzel was right; he is your mate, and you are his."

"What about Careene? She was his mate, too, and a great queen for your people." She gave her head a shake. "I can't compete with that."

"You are wrong, Robyn Earth-clan. No one expects you to compete with Careene; only to be the best you can be in your own right. Careene loved her fledglings and her clan. She *cared* for Kyzel, but there was never true love between them—only deep respect. Respect enough for her to extract a death-bed vow from him that he take his next mate for love. So, he came here to fulfill that vow, and met you. You touched him, Robyn Martin. You have a piece of him he has never, and will never, give to another. His heart."

"They'll never accept me, Rol. Your people. How could they trust a human to have their best interests at heart?" And why did a part of her ache to prove she did?

"Because love matches are rare, and they will see and honor what you share with their monarch, as I do."

She so wanted to believe that, but…. "I can't, Rol. I have people here who depend on me. Women with little hope and in desperate positions. I can't abandon them."

"As a monarch, you will be in an even better position to help them."

"From hundreds of light years away?" A huff of disbelief escaped her. "How?"

Rol dipped his chin and fixed her with a *think about it* look. "Do you know how many times I have heard the story of your first date to the bird *sanctuary*?"

"What does the sanctuary have to do…?" *Oh, my gosh. A* sanctuary.

A place of safety. A place to heal and start over without fear of being hunted down by angry exes. She could give that to them, if she followed her heart.

Wonder filled her, and she met his gaze. "Rol…that could work."

"You are in a rare position to be a monarch for both our people, kee mohap. If you will just embrace the gift before you. Please."

144

This made so much sense. More than walking away from the one love of her life. Because there would never be another who came anywhere close to stirring what she felt for Kyzel.

"Kee mohap?" That sounded so familiar. "What's that mean?"

"My monarch." Rol's smile was somewhere between knowing and smug. "Your decision is needed, as your mate will depart from the galactic spaceport soon."

Everything good came in the winged package named Kyzel. Her future, her passion, lay with this amazing, loving man. Her heart seemed to shatter within her chest, and she met Kathy's sparkling gaze. Her daughter was grinning as if she'd already figured out how her mom would respond.

Smart aleck, kid.

Damp warmth streamed over Robyn's face and she touched her fingertips to her cheeks. When had the tears started?

"Mom?"

She swallowed hard then nodded. "Help me pack, honey."

"Where is Prime Advisor Rol? A *short errand* should not take so long."

Elder Kai had a way of stating the obvious, but all Kyzel could do was give his shoulders a shrug. There was nothing left within him to make much more of a response. Not when he was moments away from leaving the birth-world of the woman he loved, and would never see again. He would be mated by the elders when he arrived home, without love. That much had been evident in the subversive looks Elder Kai had been giving him the past few days.

I am sorry, Careene.

He had done all he could, but forcing Robyn to be his mate would not be a love-based action. At least Careene's soul should not be denied entrance to Great Aerie despite his failure.

Fyad raised one hand to shield his eyes. "There he is." A giant grin lightened the male's face. "He did it! She came."

Who came? Kyzel frowned, and followed Fyad's line of sight. Indeed, through the shimmering desert air the wavering form of a Bezchian flight was visible, coming closer. And he did appear to be carrying something, or *someone*, in his arms. He blinked, shifting to hunting vision, and the scene became clear. Robyn was in his friend's arms, waving one hand while the other was hooked around Rol's neck.

She is here!

The spike of elation dimmed. But why had she come? They had said their goodbyes days ago, for what it was worth.

"We do not have time for this," Elder Kai groused. "We must go."

The rush of air from Rol's wings swirled the desert heat and sand around him. His friend's feet had barely touched the ground when Robyn wiggled out of his arms.

"*Kyzel!*"

Without a thought, he spread his arms in invitation, and she did not hesitate. Three steps and she had wrapped her arms around his middle as if she would never let go. "I'm sorry…I was stupid…don't go."

He dipped his head and inhaled her sweet scent. "I must. My duties…."

She tipped her head back. "I want to go with you."

He blinked at her, wonder filling him like sunshine. Somewhere nearby, tires squealed and car doors slammed, but it hardly mattered. If there was any danger, Fyad would take care of it.

She wants to come with me!

"Are you certain?" Just in case he had not heard correctly.

"One hundred percent."

There was no hint of doubt in her eyes. "Robyn—"

"Oh, Jesus, just say *yes*." Meryl's voice cut through his confusion.

"No." He moved his hands to Robyn's shoulders and bent until he was eye level with her. "Instead, I will say, I love you, Robyn Martin, but I will not settle for you just coming with me. I want you to be my mate in all ways."

She grinned. "Yes. For the rest of our lives, *yes*. And we're going to Bezchi."

"What about your commitments here?"

She tapped her finger against the tip of his nose. "I have a plan to talk over with you."

Then her soft full lips were on his, parting more than enough for him to explore her mouth with his tongue. To savor her sweetness, then draw her into him.

A gasp came from Elder Kai's direction. Of course, the mate-matcher would not be happy with the situation.

Rol cleared his throat, loudly. "My monarch, the ship awaits."

Kyzel pulled back and gazed into her beautiful eyes. "Go, say your good-byes, Robyn Raptorclaw. I will be patient." They had the rest of their lives, after all.

Once the hugs, tears, and promises to visit had all been made, she was back at his side, her hand in his as he led her up the ramp.

A vibration from inside his leather carrier startled him. "What is this?" He reached inside the carrier and pulled out the small device. "Oh, no."

"What?" Robyn's concerned gaze was on him.

"I forgot to leave Ms. Vogel's phone at the suite, and I think she is calling me to remind me." He flicked his finger over the screen and raised the phone to his ear. "Hello."

"Kyzel, thank God." Ms. Vogel sounded relieved. "I've been trying to get ahold of your friend, Rol with an update on his application."

"His app—"

"*Do not* let him leave. A match has been found!"

He turned his gaze toward Rol's. "A ma—"

"He can use your phone, just have him bring it over to the office at two o'clock. Oh, and we'll leave him in the same suite, too. I gotta go…have another client waiting."

The line clicked off, and Kyzel lowered the phone with a frown.

"Did you forget to return the device, kee mohap?" Rol asked.

He gave his head a shake. "Rol, you did not tell me you had applied to the Silverstar Agency."

Rol tilted his head to one side. "I did not."

Kyzel held up the cell phone. "Then why does Ms. Vogel say a match has been found for you?"

"That…that is not possible." Rol's feathers fluffed with agitation.

"I cannot imagine she would make it up."

"This is nonsense I have no time for. We are about to leave."

"*We* are, but *you* are not."

Rol opened his mouth yet nothing came out—a rare occurrence.

Kai moved his head, watching their exchange with undisguised curiosity. "I believe I shall stay too."

"I am *not* staying," Rol blurted. "I never applied; you *know* I would not. This reeks of foul play."

"Perhaps." He gave his head a slow shake. "Perhaps. However, you are a male of honor. There is too much at stake right now to jeopardize our budding relationship with Earth."

Rol's mouth trembled as though he fought to keep a flock of words inside.

"You get to stay in the same suite." Kyzel extended his arm with the phone. "Besides, this may give you the opportunity to witness the ratification of the trade agreement."

A low growl emitted from Rol's throat, and he snatched the phone. "Safe travels, my monarch."

"Thank you, Rol. May the wind be under your wings until we meet again. And, Fyad, I am entrusting the welfare of our Prime to you."

Fyad's eyes widened with surprise, then the young man grinned and inclined his head. "As you desire, kee mohap."

"Very good." And now, it was time to take Robyn home. "Robyn, my life mate, are you ready?"

Joy danced in her blue eyes. "I am so ready."

He offered her his hand. "Then let us greet this new life, this new adventure, together."

To my dear readers,

Above the Storm is my first venture into writing humorous, seasoned SFR romance. Thank you for joining me in this new universe. (((Hug))) Please let me know what you think by leaving a review.

Also, keep an eye on my website and other social media sites for excerpts and progress reports on both my Prophecy series, and my Silverstar series.

Happy reading!

~Lea Kirk

*Please turn the page
to enjoy an excerpt from*

Wing and a Prayer
Silverstar Mates

Legally speaking, Meryl Faulkner was in a gray area, and that was not a good place for a retired divorce lawyer to be. She tapped the edge of her debit card against the grocery checkout counter. The whole situation wouldn't be quite so bad if she hadn't involved her goddaughter in her crime last night. But, if that damn man—because it was *always* a man—hadn't pissed her off so royally, she would've thought things through a little more carefully. Which wasn't an excuse because the facts spoke for themselves.

The first time she'd met the giant winged Bezchian lug, Rol Raptorclaw, she'd been all sorts of turned on. What guy his age could carry off the shirtless look so flawlessly? Had such defined abs? Looked so hot in nothing but leather flying straps and black pants? And spoke in a voice that could make a woman orgasm on the spot?

And those wings—my God.

But seriously, all that yumminess didn't make up for the way he'd tried to undermine his good friend Kyzel's budding romance with her best friend, Robyn. Poor Robyn deserved a chance to find a guy who was better than that damn ex-husband of hers, Kevin. And Kyzel was *exponentially* better.

Meryl had warned Rol to back off, but had he listened? Nooo. Of course not. Instead, he'd cornered Robyn during her lunch break yesterday and done everything to make her jealous of Kyzel's dead wife.

She frowned. And speaking of Robyn, her friend hadn't followed up with her today about that incident. Maybe she should drive by on her way home from the grocery store and make sure everything was okay. It was so unusual not to hear from her.

"Ms. Faulkner? Ma'am?"

Meryl blinked, the familiar electronic beeps and buzzes of the store filtering back into her consciousness. She met the expectant brown-eyed gaze of the grocery clerk. Cute young thing with hair done in neat cornrows.

I used to be that young. And cute.

The girl waved one hand in the direction of the ancient card reader. "You can tap your card now."

"Oh, right. Sorry." She set the card over the scanner.

What was the line from that movie? *"It's not the years, it's the mileage."* Sixty-three used to seem so far away, but now here she was, retired and just a couple years away from being a senior citizen.

She slipped her card back into her purse, then stared at the back of her hand. A few age spots were there, barely visible against her brown skin. It helped that she bleached her shoulder-length curls to a light-gold color. It hid the salt and pepper that only she knew was there. Not much she could do about the crow's feet at the corners of her eyes, though. Robyn called them laugh lines, but Robyn also managed to see the best in everyone.

Or, maybe she's right.

Life had been pretty happy. Even the disaster of a marriage to Nathan had been fun, despite her scare with cervical cancer, and the resulting hysterectomy that had stolen their ability to have a family. He had been there for her, strong and reassuring, for twenty-seven years. They'd lived their happily ever after until...Charlotte. Ditzy, petite, young Charlotte Cremean with her deep brown eyes, thick dark hair, and her equally thick head.

Totally missed all the signs on that one, didn't I?

Hadn't even batted an eyelash when Nathan wanted to hire her as their new secretary. Why would she have? She'd *trusted* him. Now all she had to show for those years were scars. A puckered one on her abdomen, and invisible ones on her heart. Did she need any other reminders how men liked to play women?

Aren'tcha glad you kept your last name now?

"Here's your receipt, ma'am."

Ma'am. I'm old enough to be a ma'am.

"Thank you." She took the receipt between her fingers and jammed it into the bag with the yogurt and bananas.

"Has anyone told you that you look like Michelle Hurd?"

She clamped down on the snort trying to escape. "So often that I could apply to be her stunt double and probably get the job."

Not that anyone would hire a "ma'am"-aged woman to do that job. Much easier to hire a younger, more flexible one and do distance shots.

"You could." The girl laughed. "Have a good evening."

"You too."

Out in the parking lot, the old wheels on the grocery cart rattled, and the whole contraption shimmied. Damn thing better not fall apart on her before she got to the car. How was it that ten years after first contact was made, asphalt was still a thing? Didn't one of the other planets that belonged to the Galactic Alliance have a better surfacing solution they could share with Earth?

A whole decade, yet the first time I met an off-worlder was only a few days ago.

And what was it about Rol that kept him floating to the forefront of her thoughts all the time? The dignified gray and brown headfeathers and wings? His buff as a twenty-five-year-old's body? Which sort of made sense since a spare tire would make flying difficult. Or those eyes...one gray and one blue...that she could stare into for hours... days... months... *years*?

Dammit. Don't think about him like that!

She stopped behind her sporty little silver coupe and loaded her bags into the trunk. Rol was a dick, and she'd wronged him for it by having her goddaughter, Kathy hack into the Silverstar Agency's database, submit a fake application for him, then bio apped one of his feathers to them as well. And that damn feather was *still* in her purse. Why? Because it smelled all allspicey-warm, like Rol, and she couldn't let it go.

Who's the dick now, Meryl? Ma'am?

She rolled the empty cart into the rack. He'd be so pissed if he ever found out what she'd done to him. If she was really lucky, he'd be back on Bezchi long before the agency matched him, and the whole thing would blow over. As hard as it was to admit it, she'd let down all womankind with her petty little stunt.

And yet, just the thought of him leaving made her heart sad. It was beyond crazy, but she might be hooked on the guy, which was another thing he could never know.

She slid behind the steering wheel, the bucket seat conforming to her ass. The cheery notes of The Wedding

March came from inside her purse, and her stomach clenched. It'd seemed funny to give that ringtone to Nixy Vogel, the Silverstar agent assigned to her. Now, not so much.

This could be the call I've been dreading.

The one she'd known would eventually come the moment Robyn had coerced her into submitting an application with her. It wasn't like *she* needed a guy in her life again. Why, oh why didn't she think to have Kathy delete her application last night?

"Well, Nixy, honey, leave a message." It was getting dark, and she still wanted to drive by Robyn's to make sure her bestie was home and safe.

Anything Nixy had to tell her could wait until after the groceries were put away.

Want more out of this world love?

Hitch a ride on the Intergalactic Dating Agency's space ship to romance! Our friendly author-pilots will take you on adventures you will never forget.

Now boarding here:
RomancingTheAlien.com

About the Author

USA Today Bestselling Author Lea Kirk loves to transport her readers to other worlds with her science fiction romance books. She's the author of the award-winning Prophecy series, and the rollicking romantic Silverstar Mates series about seasoned SFR love, that's part of the Intergalactic Dating Agency series. Why? Because sexy has no expiration date!

Ms. Kirk lives in California with her wonderful hubby, their five kids (aka, the nerd herd), and a spoiled, bossy, yet somehow adorable, pup.

LeaKirk.com